Haunted Athletes

True Ghost Stories

ALLAN ZULLO

To Chad Manausa,
who I know will always give his spirited best
on the playing field

Copyright © 1997 by The Wordsellers, Inc.

Published by Troll Communications L.L.C.

All rights reserved. No part of this book may be reproduced or utilized in any form or by any means, electronic or mechanical, including photocopying, recording, or by any information storage and retrieval system, without written permission from the publisher.

Cover design by Tony Greco & Associates.

Cover illustration by Kersti Frigell.

Printed in the United States of America.

10 9 8 7 6 5 4 3 2

CONTENTS

Do Ghosts Haunt the Playing Arenas?

Athletes and fans say they have seen ghosts in all sorts of sporting arenas—on the baseball diamond, the football gridiron, the basketball court, and the soccer field.

In many cases, experts were called in to investigate these so-called hauntings. Usually the experts walked away baffled. All they knew for sure was that something weird had happened—something that could not be fully explained.

Haunted Athletes is a creepy collection of stories about athletes who have been haunted by spirits. These eerie tales are inspired, in part, by real-life cases taken from the files of noted ghost hunters. The names and places in the stories have been changed to protect everyone's privacy.

Will a ghost haunt you on the sidelines, in the dugout, or on the basketball court? You might think so after reading the spooky stories in this book!

REVENGE OF THE HAWK

As he walked gingerly through the manicured cemetery, Frankie Linquist whispered to his teammates, "Let's hurry up and get this over with. This place gives me the creeps."

"What's the matter?" taunted Jonas Habersham. "Haven't you been in a marble orchard before?"

"As a matter of fact, no," Frankie replied. "I identify more with the living than the dead."

"I don't know about that, Frankie," joked Dylan Dixon. "You always look half dead on the basketball court."

The three teens, along with Kendall Jackson and Greg Lang, formed the starting lineup for Fox Valley Academy, a private boys' prep school. They were creeping through Rolling Hills Memorial Park on a crisp fall evening to pose for pictures. Fellow student and amateur photographer Brett Gompertz had convinced them to wear their uniforms to the cemetery. He thought the gravestones would make the perfect backdrop for a Fox Valley Phantoms basketball team photo. Brett planned to place the picture in the school newspaper and on posters in all the store windows in town.

After three straight losing seasons, Brett was worried

that fans wouldn't come out to support the team this year. But since the team had a new coach and three starting seniors, Fox Valley actually had a good shot at a winning season. Brett wanted the locals to know that the Phantoms had been revived. So he hit upon a "back from the dead" theme. He wanted to create a poster featuring a photo of the starters in the graveyard along with the season schedule. The top of the poster would say "FOX VALLEY PHANTOMS 1995–96 OBITUARY PAGE" with the usual headings changed to read "Deceased" (opponents), "Entered into Rest" (date of game), "Place of Death" (location of game), and "Time of Death" (start of game).

Brett fumbled with his camera bag, tripod, and lights as he looked for a place to set up. "I need to find the right gravestone for you to pose next to," he said.

"What about this one?" asked Kendall, hugging an angel that stood on a marble block. "She looks like the date Dylan had the other night."

"Hey, guys! Over here!" shouted Greg, standing next to a six-foot-tall (1.8-m) granite marker. It resembled a miniature Washington Monument, except for the stone ball perched on top. The entire structure rested on a base of darker granite, which was engraved with the words:

JEROME KINGMAN HAWKINS
BORN: Aug. 3, 1928
DIED: July 12, 1991

"This is perfect," Brett announced. "The round stone on top looks like a basketball."

The five players crowded around the tombstone. Jonas looked at the carved name and asked, "Hawkins? Is that the same person that Hawkins Hall is named after?"

"Beats me," Greg answered.

"Let's not waste time," Frankie fretted. "I have a lot of homework."

"What's your hurry?" asked Dylan. "Enjoy the surroundings. After all, people are dying to get in here."

After setting up his equipment, Brett posed the players. "Frankie and Kendall, stand on the base, one on each side of the tombstone. Dylan and Greg, you're the shortest, so stand in the front. And Jonas, since you're the tallest, get behind the gravemarker and put your head next to the stone ball."

As Brett snapped pictures, Jonas told his teammates, "You know, it's not right for us to be crawling around Jerome Hawkins's grave. I mean, here we are posing, and below us is a dead man. What if his ghost gets angry and attacks us?"

"Get real, Jonas," Kendall scoffed.

Suddenly a loud, eerie moan echoed through the darkness. The groan grew into a seething, low voice that hissed from the ground, "Ohhhhh, what are you doing to my grave?"

"Whoa, man, who's saying that?" Frankie gasped.

"Ohhhhh, you will suffer the consequences," the voice threatened.

"I'm outta here!" Frankie declared. He started to jump off the base of the marker, but Jonas reached around the monument and grabbed Frankie by the wrist. "Stay here with us, Frankie," Jonas said. "There's safety in numbers. We'll fight this ghost together."

"Let me go!" Frankie shouted.

Frankie struggled with his teammate until he broke free. But in the tussle, they accidentally knocked the stone ball

7

off the monument. The ball struck the base, chipping a corner, and then split in two. Frankie sprinted off into the night.

"Now look what we've done," groaned Jonas.

"Look what *we've* done?" protested Kendall. "You're the one who came up with the scheme to scare Frankie. You're the one who secretly placed the tape recorder behind the tree and turned it on. You're the one who knocked off the ball."

"It was an accident," said Jonas. "I didn't mean for this to happen. What are we going to do now?"

Kendall turned to Brett. "Do you have all the shots you need?"

"Yeah, I guess so," Brett replied.

"Okay, then, let's split."

"Wait," countered Brett. "We can't leave this mess here."

Greg raised his hands in a calming gesture. "If everyone stays cool, we might be able to save our skins. We'll write an anonymous letter of apology and send it to the cemetery along with the money to have the monument fixed."

"What about my photos?" asked Brett.

"Trash the photos," snapped Kendall. "You can't use them now—they'll prove we were responsible for damaging the tombstone."

"But what about my poster idea?" Brett protested. "My back-from-the-dead theme—"

"You'll just have to come up with a different idea," said Dylan. "Now let's get out of here."

The four players scurried off, leaving Brett standing alone by the tombstone. As he slowly gathered his things, he heard an eerie moan—creepier than the one before—

that seemed to be coming from under the earth. Brett jumped back in surprise. Then he relaxed and smiled. *It's just Jonas's tape recorder,* he thought. *He probably forgot to take it with him.*

Brett walked to a nearby marble gravestone, where he had seen Jonas hide the tape recorder. But the recorder was gone.

Then he heard the moan again. It was so unearthly, so chilling, that Brett began to shiver. *What's the matter with me? It has to be one of the guys. I won't give them the satisfaction of scaring me like they did Frankie.*

Suddenly a muffled voice dripping with malice rumbled, "I . . . won't . . . forget."

"I won't forget either," Brett said with a sarcastic laugh. Assuming his friends were watching, Brett strolled out of the cemetery as if nothing was the matter. However, his legs and heart urged him to move fast, because there was always the chance that the voice came from the grave of Jerome Kingman Hawkins—whoever he was.

When he got back to the dormitory, Brett went straight to Jonas's room and asked, "Do you have your tape recorder?"

"Yeah, it's right under my bed. Why?"

"Just checking."

The other players filed into Jonas's room. They made a pact not to tell another living soul about what had happened in the cemetery, and each one tossed twenty dollars onto Jonas's bed to help pay for the damage to the gravemarker. "I'll write the letter and tell them it was an accident," said Greg.

At that moment, a cold draft swept into the room, scattering the money in all directions. "Hey," said Dylan, "close the—" He stopped in mid-sentence when they all noticed that the window was already closed. So was the door.

"Do any of you have a good explanation for what happened here and at the cemetery?" Frankie asked. The others shook their heads. They weren't ready to confess they had tricked him at the cemetery. But they also had no clue to the source of the draft.

After several seconds of silence, Frankie announced, "Well then, this is my cue to split."

Frankie hurried back to his room and climbed into bed. But he was unable to fall asleep. He just couldn't get the spooky thought of ghosts out of his mind. "Did I really hear a ghost or did those guys play a joke on me?" he asked himself. "If I were a ghost, I'd be upset if kids were jumping on my gravestone. And what about the cold draft in Jonas's room? I read that a room will get chilly when a ghost is present. Could it have been Hawkins's ghost?"

Frankie became aware of halting footsteps in the hallway. They weren't the soft padding of a student on his way to the bathroom. These steps were the slow plodding of an old man. Frankie got up and cracked open his door, expecting to see someone. But the hallway was empty.

Nevertheless, the footsteps continued down the hall— right toward his room. Frankie rubbed his eyes and slapped his face to make sure he was awake. The footsteps stopped in front of Dylan's door. Frankie looked on in disbelief as Dylan's doorknob turned to the left and to the right by itself.

"Oh, my gosh!" he gasped under his breath. "Oh, my gosh!"

Frankie listened in fascinated horror as the footsteps moved to Jonas's room. Again, the doorknob turned left and right. The eerie sequence was repeated at Greg's, Brett's, and Kendall's doors.

"It's the ghost!" Frankie uttered to himself. "He's coming to my room next! Do I go or stay? Stay for what? Get out of here!"

Frankie ducked into the stairwell next to his room and streaked down the stairs. But in his panicky haste, he lost his balance and tumbled the final six steps to the bottom of the landing. When he tried to stand up, he yelped from the sharp pain in his left ankle. He couldn't put any weight on his left foot.

"Oh, no, not my ankle," Frankie whimpered. "Not an injury a week before the season starts." Groaning, he hobbled up the stairs on one foot. When he reached the top of the landing, he stood still, waiting to hear any footsteps. To his great relief, the hallway was quiet.

The next day, Frankie's swollen, black-and-blue ankle was examined by the team physician. "You've suffered a severe sprain, Frankie," said the doctor. "You'll be on crutches for about a week before you can put any weight on it. I'm afraid you'll miss the first three weeks of the season."

"The ghost!" Frankie muttered to himself. "He did this to me!"

"Pardon?"

"Doc, I don't expect you to understand. But it's pay-back time—and I think I just got paid back."

Meanwhile, in the school darkroom, Brett had finished

developing the roll of film he had taken at the cemetery. He decided to print up the best ones and take a look at them before he destroyed them. He didn't want the pictures to be used as evidence against the players or him, but Brett didn't see the harm in looking at the prints in the privacy of the darkroom.

But when he took the negatives out of the pan of developing solution, Brett pounded his fist on the counter in disgust.

"This sucks!" he complained. Every frame of the boys posing on Jerome Hawkins's gravestone showed an unexpected streak of light next to them.

Brett printed up several pictures to get a better look at the streak. He was surprised to discover that the light grew bigger with each photo he had shot in sequence. In the final picture, the light had grown into the shape and size of a person.

That's odd, Brett thought. *It's not a normal streak of light. It looks like white smoke. Maybe there's something wrong with my camera.*

Brett inserted a new roll of film into the camera and went over to the gym to take shots of basketball practice. After snapping twelve shots, Brett returned to the darkroom and processed the film. It came out fine. *There's nothing wrong with the camera*, Brett said to himself. *Which means . . . what?* A shiver wound its way up his back. He stuffed the graveyard photos in his backpack and left the darkroom.

That evening, Brett asked the five players to meet him in his room. Jonas was the first to arrive.

"Jonas, you look terrible!" Brett exclaimed when he saw

Jonas's bloodshot eyes and flushed face. "Did you have a bad practice today?"

"No. Tanya dumped me. Can you believe it? She dumped me for some pipsqueak at Central High. I'm so angry, I'd like to kick some butt."

"I'm sorry, Jonas. But I've got something that should take your mind off Tanya."

When the others assembled, Brett said, "I want to show you something totally bizarre." He whipped out the photos. "Look at these shots and tell me what you think the white thing is."

"Kind of ghostly, if you ask me," said Greg.

"Yeah," added Dylan. "You can sort of make out a head and shoulders and body."

Frankie's eyes grew wide. "That proves it! That proves it!"

"Proves what, Frankie?" Kendall asked.

"What we heard in the cemetery last night was a ghost!"

"That was no—oof," said Greg, as Kendall elbowed him in the ribs to shut him up.

"Laugh if you want to," Frankie said, "but the ghost was here last night. I heard his footsteps and I saw the doorknobs of each of your rooms turn by themselves."

"Are you sure you weren't dreaming?" asked Greg.

"No! It was real. That's when I went out to investigate and fell down the stairs."

When the others started to snicker, Frankie flushed with anger. "Open the door for me, will you? I gotta get out of here," he mumbled and tottered out of the room on his crutches.

Kendall and Jonas waited as long as they could before

bursting out laughing. "Frankie still doesn't know about the tape recorder," roared Jonas. "He thinks there really was a ghost. Isn't that wild?"

Kendall patted Brett on the back. "Man, Frankie is freaking out. Can you believe he thinks a ghost visited the dorm? Now these photos have absolutely convinced him a ghost is haunting us. Brett, how did you doctor the photos?"

Brett shook his head. "I didn't fake these shots. I don't know what the white streak is. There's nothing wrong with the film or my camera."

"But we didn't see anything," noted Dylan.

"There's something I need to know," Brett said. "When you guys left the cemetery, did any of you sneak back and try to scare me?"

"No, we came straight back to campus," replied Kendall.

"After you four left, I heard an eerie voice that seemed to be coming from the grave."

"You sound just like Frankie." Jonas chuckled.

Brett held up his hand. "I'm not saying this is a photo of a ghost. But you have to admit, it's weird."

"Greg," asked Kendall, "have you written the letter of apology yet?"

"No, but I'll get around to it."

Later that night, Jonas was heading down the hall from the bathroom when he heard slow, plodding footsteps behind him. He stopped and turned around, but didn't see anyone. Nervous, he scurried to his room and shut the door.

Moments later, there was a knock on the door. "Wh-who's there?" he stammered. The only response was another knock.

Jonas grabbed a baseball bat and held it high in his left hand as he cautiously opened the door with his right hand. He peered outside but didn't see anyone in the hallway. He closed the door, then turned around—and gasped in surprise.

Hovering in the middle of the room was a smoky white form in the shape of a human. The shimmering figure began to float toward him.

Jonas gripped his bat with both his hands. "Stay away from me, whatever you are!" he shouted. The smoky figure moved closer.

A wave of panic swept over him, and Jonas lashed out at the unearthly intruder. The bat sliced through the phantom and crashed down on Jonas's table, breaking it in two. But the specter's form didn't change. It swayed to the right when Jonas took another vicious swing. The bat had no effect on the ghost, but shattered a desk lamp and cracked Jonas's desk. The ghostly form bobbed to the left and to the right as Jonas bashed away in the darkness.

The crashing noise woke up the other students. They hurried into the room and turned on the light. Jonas was still swinging his bat, battering everything around him.

"Jonas!" shouted Dylan. "What are you doing?"

His face dripping with sweat and his chest heaving, the wild-eyed boy stopped swinging and let the bat fall to the floor.

"Jonas, you've destroyed your room!" said Kendall. The arms on Jonas's upended chair were in splinters. His desk and table had caved in from the beating. Holes pockmarked two walls, and books had been knocked helter-skelter.

"The ghost was in my room!" Jonas stammered. "He was trying to attack me! You saw him, didn't you?"

The other players looked at one another and shook their heads. Dylan went over and led Jonas to the bed. "You'd better calm down. You're taking this breakup with Tanya a little too hard, don't you think?"

"It was the ghost."

"Yeah, whatever." Dylan surveyed the room. "There's no way we can fix any of this. You are in big trouble."

Dylan was right. The next day, the headmaster concluded that Jonas was so upset over losing his girlfriend, he took out his anger on his room. "You will pay for the damages to your room and you will be suspended from the basketball team for two weeks," the headmaster pronounced.

When Coach Dwight Davidson learned that he had now lost his second starter in two days, he threw the basketball down in disgust. "This is just great," he thundered. "What else can go wrong?"

He found out soon enough.

Dylan, whose grades were borderline at best, needed to turn in an overdue report for English class. He worked late into the night, typing hunt-and-peck style on his computer. His eyelids felt like lead and his back ached. Time after time, he found himself nodding off.

Dylan looked at his watch. *It's 2:30 in the morning and I still need to write another two pages. What's that noise? Footsteps. Someone is in the hall.* Dylan was too tired to get up. He turned his attention back to the computer.

Dylan had just started typing again when he noticed a strange reflection on the computer screen. It looked like the smoky figure in Brett's photographs. Dylan spun around in his chair, but he didn't see anything behind him. *I must be imagining things. I'm so tired . . . so tired . . .*

Dylan opened his eyes, but his mind was still fuzzy. His head was resting on the keyboard. *Oh, no. I fell asleep! What time is it?* He focused on his watch and let out a yell of frustration. *It's almost eight in the morning! If I don't finish this report, I'm toast! Hey, why isn't my report on the screen?*

Dylan hit a couple of keys to call up his paper. But the computer screen flashed "CANNOT FIND FILE." *Where's my report? It's got to be here!* Dylan thought frantically. He called up every directory and checked every file, but his work was nowhere to be found.

Dylan failed the first grading period in English class because he hadn't turned in the report by the extended deadline. As a result, he was ineligible to play on the team—the third straight blow to the Fox Valley Phantoms and Coach Davidson.

By now the coach was so numb from all the bad news that he half-expected more to follow. It did.

The night after Dylan was ruled ineligible, Greg and Kendall were horsing around in the dormitory hall with a basketball. One player would dribble while the other tried to take the ball away from him without fouling. If the dribbler could maintain possession of the ball for ten seconds, he got a point. If the defender stole the ball, he got the point.

While the two exchanged trash talk, Greg dribbled with the skill of a seasoned guard, keeping the ball away from Kendall. Suddenly Greg was astounded to see a ghostly form emerging from the wall. Kendall, whose eyes were glued to the ball, slapped it out of Greg's hands. Kendall lunged forward to grab the ball, and his head slammed into Greg's with a sickening thud.

The players tumbled to the floor, dazed. Unable to move, they watched the ghostly figure hover over them for several seconds before it slipped back through the wall and vanished.

Greg and Kendall were taken to the hospital, where the doctor determined they both had suffered slight concussions. They were ordered to rest for a few days before starting practice again. That meant they would miss the first two games.

With all five starters out of the lineup, the Fox Valley Phantoms began the season by getting crushed 46–23 and 59–24.

As the players showered after their second loss, Coach Davidson leaned against the locker room wall and muttered to a reporter, "It's going to be a long, long season. I haven't felt this helpless since Old Man Hawkins had me fired."

Brett, who was standing next to the reporter, perked up at the mention of Hawkins's name. He asked the coach, "Old Man Hawkins?"

"Yeah, he's the bigwig your dormitory is named after," the coach replied. "He went to school here a long time ago. Everyone called him The Hawk. He was the richest man in town. He was also the meanest. Back in 1982, The Hawk didn't like the way I was coaching, so he went to the administration and told them he would donate the money for a new dormitory if they would fire me. They took all of two seconds to decide—and they sent me packing. Then in 1991, The Hawk died and a new administration came in. I was hired back this year."

Brett gnawed his lower lip and asked, "What was Hawkins's first name?"

"Jerome."

Back at the dormitory, Brett found the players gathered in Greg's room. When Brett told them who Jerome Hawkins was, they were convinced The Hawk's ghost was harassing them.

"Everything bad that's happened to us came after we fooled around on Hawkins's tombstone," said Frankie. "We all know Hawkins's ghost is to blame for our problems. I hurt my ankle because of him."

Jonas cleared his throat. "I didn't destroy my room because Tanya ditched me. I saw a ghost in my room—the same one in Brett's photos. I was trying to beat the ghost with my bat, but I kept hitting everything but him."

Dylan spoke up next. "I'm sure the ghost erased the report on my computer when I dozed off."

"Kendall and I saw the ghost hovering over us in the hallway when we collided," added Greg. "Hawkins's ghost must be sore at us for busting his tombstone. He's the one responsible for knocking us out of the lineup."

"Greg," asked Brett, "did you send the money to the cemetery yet?"

"Well, uh, I've been so busy with homework and practice that I . . . um . . . sorry, guys."

"Write it right now," Jonas demanded. "We're not leaving this room until you've written that letter. We may never play hoops again if we don't apologize."

"Yeah, and Fox Valley may never win another game unless the tombstone gets fixed," added Kendall.

Greg sat at his computer and banged out a short note that read:

> To Whom It May Concern:
> While in Rolling Hills Memorial Park, we were admiring the gravestone of Jerome Hawkins when we accidentally knocked off the stone ball on top of his monument.
> Enclosed is $120 to pay for the repair to the gravestone.
> We meant no disrespect and we apologize to Mr. Hawkins's family and especially to his spirit. Please accept our deepest regrets for the accident.

After the letter was mailed, the players took turns walking by the cemetery every day to see if the gravestone had been fixed. Two weeks passed without any repairs. Meanwhile, the Phantoms kept losing, even when the original starters began returning to the lineup.

It came as no surprise to Brett and the starters when Fox Valley Academy finally won its first basketball game of the season. It happened on the very day that a new stone ball was affixed on top of Jerome Hawkins's tombstone.

THE PROMISE

Tony Ballardi rubbed his sweaty palms on a towel as his eyes focused on the pins at the end of the alley. *All I need is seventeen to beat Norris,* thought the fifteen-year-old bowler. *If I can't get seventeen in the final frame, I don't deserve to be here.*

Tony picked up his bowling ball, crouched, and went through the same routine he always did—he pictured all the pins falling. Then, in one fluid motion, he rolled the ball. His hard hook hugged the very edge of the gutter before making a sweeping curve right into the pocket. The pins flew in all directions. A strike!

The crowd in the stands broke into applause. Above the clapping, Tony heard a voice familiar to him at all his tournaments. "Attaboy, Tony! Attaboy!" The cheer came from his number-one fan—his grandfather, Carmine Gallo.

Tony smiled at him and swaggered back to the ball return. *I have this one in the bag,* he thought. *I have two balls left to pick up seven pins. I can do this with my eyes closed.* He confidently plucked his ball from the return, winked at his grandfather, and got ready. Then he had a brilliant idea.

Why not throw with my eyes closed? People will go nuts. I'll be a legend at fifteen. Imagine, tossing the winning shot with my eyes closed at the Bowling Quarterly Teen Regional Championship. I've got to do it.

Tony closed his eyes and turned his head just enough so that some of the crowd could see what he was doing. He wanted to make sure that Norris saw him. A surprised murmur spread throughout the spectators. Then Tony took his three steps and let the ball fly. But the moment the ball smacked onto the wood with a dull thud, he regretted ever doing this lamebrained stunt.

Not following through on his routine cost him dearly. The ball strayed right, hovered on the edge of the channel, and then, to Tony's horror, tumbled into the gutter. The crowd gasped so loud, Tony felt as though they had sucked all the air out of the bowling center.

All of Tony's confidence went bounding down that gutter. *How could I have been so stupid?* he thought as a wave of nausea swept over him. He wanted to look at his grandfather, to gaze into those warm, brown, puppy-dog eyes and get reassurance. But Tony was too embarrassed to face him.

"Tony, Tony, Tony," yelled Carmine. "Make it happen!"

Tony felt the back of his neck heat up from the shame he had brought on himself. Now he had to make one of the most important shots of his amateur bowling career. *Do I play it safe? Should I roll it down the middle or should I go with my hook—the ball that got me here in the first place?* For the first time in the tournament, Tony didn't know what to do. He wanted so desperately to talk it over with his grandfather, but of course he couldn't—not after the witless act he had just pulled.

Sweat poured down from his wristbands. Nervously, Tony wiped his hands on the towel over and over again. He never took this long to bowl. He gulped and stole a quick glance over at his competitor. Brad Norris flashed a grin that clearly said, "You're going to choke."

"Tony, Tony, Tony," yelled Carmine. "Make it happen."

Tony took a deep breath, went to the line, and tried to roll the ball safely down the middle. But he guided the ball too much. It traveled so straight that it missed the pocket and hit the head pin. The ball, with no action on it, rolled through like a bulldozer flattening trees in its path, but it didn't touch the pins on either side. Tony had knocked down only six pins, leaving behind the embarrassing "Big Ears" split—the 4-6-7-10. Even worse, he had lost the match—and the tournament—by one lousy pin.

The gallery behind him gasped in shock. A surprised Norris leaped out of his seat in joy as his supporters whooped and hollered. Biting his lower lip and blinking back tears, Tony forced himself to look at the crowd. His buddies, relatives, and mother sat stunned. His grandfather was nowhere in sight.

Tony didn't know what to say. He felt so ashamed. He stormed off the lane and through the crowd, heading for the bathroom. But before he reached the door, a meaty hand grabbed him by the arm.

"Papa," groaned Tony, "I'm so sorry. I blew it!"

"Tony, you get back out there," Carmine ordered. "Act like a man. Accept what happened and learn from it. We'll talk later."

"But, Papa—"

"Go, on. Get back there."

"Yes, Papa."

Tony reluctantly returned to the lane, where the bowling center owner and a representative from *Bowling Quarterly* magazine were presenting the trophies. Those ten minutes were the longest of Tony's life. He wanted to run away so he wouldn't have to plaster a fake smile on his face and shake hands with Norris, a guy Tony knew didn't deserve to win. *All those people are looking at me like I'm an idiot,* thought Tony. *And what about Papa? How can I face him after all that he's done for me? He must be so disappointed.*

"And for finishing second in the tournament, Tony Ballardi, we present you with this trophy," said the bowling center owner. Tony mumbled a less than heartfelt thank-you that was cut short when he heard a commotion near the men's bathroom.

"Is there a doctor in the house?" shouted a woman. "A man has collapsed. Call 911."

Then Tony heard a shriek. He could tell it was his mother screaming. Tony plowed through the crowd and saw his grandfather, pale and sweaty, sitting against the wall, clutching his heart.

"Papa, what's wrong?" Tony cried, kneeling down next to Carmine.

"I'm okay," Carmine replied weakly. "It's nothing. Bad indigestion. You know how the hot dogs are here."

"It's my fault, Papa. I caused this. I was so stupid. I was—"

"Tony, stop that talk. I'll be fine. You had nothing to do with this. I brought it on myself."

The paramedics took Carmine to the hospital, where doctors determined that the elderly man had suffered angina—pain in the heart—but not a heart attack.

The next day, Tony and his mother brought Carmine home from the hospital. Carmine had been living with them ever since Tony was ten, the worst year of the boy's life. Tony's parents had gone through a bitter divorce and his grandmother—Carmine's wife Sophia—had passed away. The only good thing to come out of those heartbreaking events was that Papa had moved into the household.

Papa, bald everywhere except for a wispy tuft of gray curls that ringed the back of his head, liked to wear the same thing every day—brown pants, a white long-sleeved shirt with the cuffs rolled up, and black suspenders. He always had a smile on his face. But it was hard to smile after the death of his beloved wife.

Meanwhile, Tony began overeating to compensate for his losses. He quickly put on fifteen extra pounds (6.75 kg).

The hurting boy and the lonely old man soon discovered they needed each other. They became very close, playing cards, watching sports on TV, and talking politics, which was Papa's passion.

One wintry day, they tried something new—bowling. Papa had a great time, even though he threw at least one gutter ball in every frame. But Tony showed a surprising talent for the sport, rolling three strikes and two spares in his first game to break 100.

"Papa, I like this game," said Tony. "Can we come back here next week?"

"Sure, Tony. You're good at this."

It soon became a ritual on Saturday mornings for Papa

to take Tony bowling. And while the old man never improved, Tony kept getting better and better. He was a born bowler.

Although Carmine didn't know anything about the sport, he worked with Tony to sharpen the boy's game. The elderly man went to the library and brought home books on bowling. He sent away for bowling videos. He sought advice from other bowlers and studied the professionals on television.

When Tony was twelve, the bowling center announced it was holding a tournament for kids. "Do you think I'm good enough to enter in the tournament, Papa?" Tony asked.

"Good enough? You're the best bowler I've ever seen! But you shouldn't sign up for the tournament."

"Why not?"

Papa chuckled and replied, "Because I already entered for you."

With Carmine's encouragement and support, Tony won first place in his age group. By now, Tony was hooked on bowling and practiced every chance he got, with his grandfather keeping score. The two began traveling to bowling centers in other towns so Tony could compete in tournaments. On those long drives, their bond grew stronger than ever. And by the time Tony was fourteen, he was the regional junior champion with an impressive average of 175.

Carmine could never sit still at a tournament in which his grandson competed. Instead, the old man would walk back and forth behind the area where the spectators sat. He would stop when Tony went into his delivery. Once the ball was released, Carmine would yell his favorite chant, "Attaboy, Tony! Attaboy!"

Often at one of the tournaments, another bowler would ask Tony, "Who's the old guy who's always with you?"

Tony would grin proudly and reply, "Oh, he's my biggest fan. I don't go anywhere without him."

Although Carmine seldom picked up a bowling ball, he developed a keen eye for the fine points of the game. He didn't hesitate to tell Tony how he could improve. At home, following the bowling sessions, the pair spent hours discussing Tony's latest game.

That's why it hurt Tony so badly when he blew the *Bowling Quarterly* tournament. He had let his grandfather down.

"Papa, I'm so sorry," Tony apologized over lunch on the day Carmine came home from the hospital. "I screwed up royally. My bowling ball has more brains than—"

"Enough, Tony!" declared Carmine, waving his hands. "Quit beating yourself up. Make what happened a positive experience."

"How?"

"Ask yourself, 'What can I learn from this?'"

"Well, for starters, I was overly confident. I'll never take anything for granted, no matter how easy it looks."

"Good. What else?"

"I forgot to go through my routine. I didn't visualize the ball going into the pocket. I didn't concentrate or follow through. I'll always remember to do those things before every throw. And I'll never forget how awful I felt when I lost."

Carmine clapped his hands in approval. "Bravo, Tony.

Look at all the things you've learned from that one bad experience." Carmine leaned back in his chair and snapped his suspenders. "Now that you learned those things, you'll be a better bowler. I wouldn't be surprised if you tossed a perfect game."

"Papa, most pros have never rolled a 300 in their life. The odds are like 50,000 to one."

"Tony, I give you my word that I will see you throw a game of nothing but strikes."

"Do you plan on living to be 150?"

"No. It will happen sooner than you think—maybe even your next tournament."

"My next tournament is the ABC Regionals. I'll be competing against the top amateur bowlers in a ten-state area. And that includes Norris and others better than him." Tony closed his eyes and winced. "How will I ever face them after my disaster? I can hear them now sticking it to me about my gutter ball."

Carmine put his arm around his grandson and said, "You know, Tony, humor can do wonders to tame a crowd— and your opponents."

"How?"

Carmine winked. "Think about it during your practice throws at the tournament."

Tony was uncommonly nervous when he arrived for the ABC Regionals. But once he toed the line for his first game, he relaxed. All he had to do was look behind him. There, pacing behind the seats, was Papa yelling, "Attaboy, Tony! Attaboy!"

Tony started out strong and fell into a groove. Concentrating and visualizing on every toss, he rolled better than his average and knocked off two adults to advance in the tourney. To his delight—and Carmine's—Tony reached the finals by blowing away Norris, 208–176. Now Tony faced Lou Nowicki, a thirty-five-year-old shoe salesman with a reputation for psyching out opponents.

As Tony and Lou shook hands at the warm-up, Lou grinned and bellowed loud enough so the spectators could hear, "So you're the young man who blew the last tournament by rolling a gutter ball. For your sake, I hope you don't do it again." The crowd tittered at his remark.

Tony looked over his shoulder and spotted his grandfather, pacing and clapping his hands. "Attaboy, Tony! Attaboy! You know what to do."

Tony stepped up to the line, went into his delivery, and fired his first warm-up toss. The ball promptly shot right into the channel. Before anyone could react, Tony announced to Lou and the crowd, "That was for all you people who missed my infamous toss in the final frame at the last tournament."

The spectators burst out laughing and applauded while Lou faked a smile. Lou's psych-out attempt had backfired. The reaction from the crowd gave Tony a boost.

"Attaboy, Tony! Attaboy!"

Surging with confidence, Tony won the first game by seven pins. But Lou came back to capture the next game by an identical margin. The championship would go to the winner of the third game.

Tony nailed two strikes to start the game. But Lou did too. The scores stayed close for most of the match. The tension mounted as they entered the ninth frame with Lou up by fifteen pins, 210–195. But then Lou faltered when he slipped on his delivery while trying for a spare. His ball tapped the 10 pin, but the pin failed to fall.

This was Tony's chance to take the lead. He turned to his grandfather, heard the words of encouragement, and then rolled a strike.

"Attaboy, Tony! Attaboy!"

In the tenth and final frame, Lou put the pressure on Tony by getting a "turkey"—three straight strikes. Lou finished with a score of 249.

Tony needed a strike if he was to have any chance of winning. He looked at his grandfather, who kept clapping and pacing. Tony went through his mental routine and then fired a strike. But he still needed one more to take control of the match. Fighting off a touch of worry, he rolled his second strike of the frame as the place erupted in cheers.

Tony was at 245 and had one more ball to throw. He took a couple of deep breaths and tried not to be too anxious or cocky. All he needed was at least five pins to win. But the last time he was in the almost identical situation, it ended in disaster. And there was another concern: Tony had never bowled higher than 225 in tournament play. Here he was, on the verge of rolling over 250. Could he do it?

"Don't choke, kid," hissed Lou.

Tony glanced behind the crowd and spotted his grandfather, walking back and forth, flashing a smile that said, "You can do it!"

Tony drew confidence from Carmine. *Don't worry, Papa,* Tony thought. *I'm not going to blow this one.*

"Better play it safe, kid," warned Lou.

No, Tony told himself, *I'm going to throw the same way I've always been throwing. I'm not going to change.*

Tony stepped to the line, went through his routine, and let the ball fly. It hugged the channel and then curved toward the pocket. Even before it hit the pins, Papa was jumping up and down, yelling, "Attaboy, Tony! Attaboy!"

Nine pins toppled over, leaving only the 7 pin standing. But it didn't matter. Tony had scored a personal high of 254 and won the biggest tournament of his life.

He marched off the lane and into the crowd of well-wishers until he found his grandfather. The old man hugged him and planted a big kiss on the boy's cheek. "I knew you could do it!" Carmine shouted gleefully. "You knew you could do it! I'm so proud of you, Tony!"

"Oh, Papa, thanks for believing in me. This is the greatest moment of my life! A 254!"

Papa's broad smile suddenly turned into a grimace. His face turned pale and he broke out into a sweat.

"Papa, are you all right?" Tony asked.

"It's nothing, Tony. It's all the excitement. I'm fine." He leaned on Tony as they walked back through the crowd. Carmine sat down by the scorer's table and drank a glass of water. Color slowly returned to his face. Then he proudly watched his grandson receive a trophy and get pinned with a gold medal that named him the top amateur bowler in the region.

That evening, over a belly-busting spaghetti dinner, Tony celebrated with his relatives. "To the best bowler in the region!" toasted Papa. "And I'll say in public what I said to you in private: Tony, you're destined for great things—including a perfect game."

"Maybe someday, Papa. Someday."

"It'll be sooner than you think. And I stick by my promise that I'll see you throw that 300."

Tragically, those were among the last words spoken by Carmine Gallo. That night, he died of a massive heart attack in his sleep. Tony had lost his biggest booster and best friend. The boy cried for two days.

At the wake, after everyone had left the funeral home, the devastated teen stood beside the casket for one last look at Papa. The heartbroken boy had no more tears left in him. He stared at his beloved grandfather and recalled all those great moments they had shared at the bowling centers: the wintry nights when Papa would drive him to the lanes; the sessions when they discussed bowling techniques over chocolate milkshakes; the tournaments when he'd hear Papa's encouraging words.

"Every promise you made to me, you kept, Papa," said Tony, looking fondly at his grandfather. "Every promise but one. You never saw me roll a perfect game. And without you there, I guess I never will. Still, you did see me win my biggest tournament. I couldn't have done it without you."

Tony unclasped the gold ABC Regionals medal from his shirt. He turned to the funeral director, held up the medal, and said, "Mr. Fazio, pin this on Papa's suit, will you please?"

"Are you sure, Tony? You just won that. You know you'll never see it again."

"It's one of the most valuable things I own," said Tony. "But I want Papa to have it for all the things he did for me. He earned it as much as I did. He deserves to have it with him forever. I know what I'm doing, and I want this medal to be buried with Papa."

A week after the funeral, the still-grieving teen walked into the kitchen and told his mother, "I'm giving up tournament bowling."

"Why would you do that, Tony?"

"I've never bowled without Papa behind me. Not having him there would be like bowling with the wrong ball or the wrong shoes. It wouldn't feel right."

Tony's mother wiped her hands on her apron, closed one eye, pursed her lips, and asked, "Now what do you suppose Papa would say if he were here right now and heard you?"

Tony looked down at his feet and replied, "I don't know. Maybe he'd tell me to go out and do my best, that I have a talent and great love for bowling, but—"

"There are no buts, Tony," retorted his mother. "You're a bowler. That's what you do best. You can't stop now simply because he's gone. Besides, he already entered you in the Lambert Lanes Open."

"How can I bowl without him? He was my biggest booster."

"Oh, and what am I? And what are your aunts, uncles, cousins, and friends? Extras in a silent movie?"

"You know what I mean, Mom."

"So what makes you think Papa won't be with you?"

"If only he could," Tony replied wistfully.

When he arrived for the tournament, Tony felt empty inside. He accepted the other bowlers' condolences over Carmine's death and their congratulations on winning the regionals. But his mind couldn't stay centered on bowling.

He kept looking behind him, wishing he could see his grandfather. He did manage to smile when his mother and relatives went overboard in their cheering for him.

After tossing his practice throws, Tony told himself, *Okay, it's time to focus on bowling. Papa, if you're out there, please look after me. I need you.*

Tony felt that same warm comfortable feeling he always had whenever he saw Papa in the crowd. A burst of self-assurance flowed through his veins as he opened the first frame. He watched the ball roll into the sweet spot and scatter all ten pins.

"That's my boy!" yelled his mother, waving her arms and jumping up and down in her seat. "Way to go, Tony!"

He rolled another strike, and then a third, fourth, and fifth straight one. He felt in a perfect groove—a zone that athletes rarely enter, where body and mind work in perfect harmony, when skill and talent reach the ultimate level. The bowling center buzzed with excitement. Could this overweight fifteen-year-old boy bowl a perfect game—twelve strikes in a row?

As Tony stepped onto the approach in the sixth frame, the place fell eerily silent. Bowlers on the other lanes waited respectfully. Waitresses tiptoed by with their trays. But once his ball was safely on its way, shouts from the spectators broke the quiet. The crash of the pins—all ten of them—triggered cheers and applause.

For a brief moment Tony thought he heard a familiar voice: "Attaboy, Tony. Attaboy!"

Tony's heart began to race. He scanned the spectators, searching for what he knew was impossible—the sight of his grandfather.

I must be imagining it, Tony thought. *I'm so used to hearing him.*

In the seventh frame, Tony rolled another strike. Once again, the crowd cheered. And once again, he heard that voice—only this time it was louder.

Tony wheeled around. There, pacing behind the crowd, was a clear but soft image of Papa! He was in his brown pants, white shirt with rolled-up sleeves, and black suspenders. The treasured ABC Regionals gold medal was pinned to his shirt.

"Attaboy, Tony! Attaboy!"

"Papa?" Tony whispered. "Is that really you?"

Papa smiled, nodded, and clapped his hands.

Tony wanted to rush through the crowd, grab his grandfather, and hug him. But Tony was afraid that if he did, the ghostly image would fade away.

Tony turned back to the alley and stepped up to the approach. *Papa is here to see me get that perfect game! Now I know I'm gonna get it!*

In the eighth frame, Tony's ball scattered all the pins except the 10 pin. It wobbled but didn't fall at first. A gasp echoed through the crowd and Tony sank to his knees in crushing disappointment. But then the spinning 7 pin skidded over and knocked down the 10. His perfect game was still alive!

Tony turned around to the crowd. He wiped his forehead and grinned. "Papa," he mouthed silently, "did you give me a little help on that one?"

The ghostly image smiled and winked.

The ninth frame was a repeat of the previous eight— another strike. Now Tony faced the pressure-packed final frame. He needed three more strikes for that coveted perfect game.

"You know what to do, Tony," said Papa's ghostly image. "So go do it!"

Tony wiped his hands on his towel. He stared at the pins. Then he went into his pre-delivery routine and launched the ball. Strike! The crowd roared its approval.

"Two more!" yelled his uncle Babe from the audience.

"Just two more!" echoed his mother.

Above the cheers, Tony heard Papa's voice say, "No, Tony. One more. Just concentrate on this one. Put everything else out of your mind."

Trying hard to keep his knees from shaking, Tony focused on the pins, visualized the toss he wanted to make, and calmly rolled his ball. It hooked beautifully into the pocket for his eleventh straight strike. One more strike and Tony would have his 300 game.

The shouting from the crowd was louder than ever. Over the din of the spectators, Tony clearly heard Papa say, "This is why I'm here, Tony. One more, just like all the others. You can do it."

Tony could feel his body tense up. He took several deep breaths, trying to calm his wildly beating heart. *I can nail it. Papa is here. And he promised to see me get my perfect game.* An incredible calm swept over him as he heard the comforting words of his grandfather: "You're going to do it."

All the pressure and doubts about making that last difficult shot vanished from Tony's mind. He was ready.

The moment Tony released the ball, everyone shouted at once, as if their yells could somehow direct the ball into the pocket. But Tony and everyone else flinched when the ball smacked high on the head pin. Some people began to groan, convinced that the perfect game was lost. But the head pin leaped out of the pack, ricocheted off the side wall, and hit the 4 pin. Seven more pins tumbled. Only one pin remained, the 9 pin. It swayed for a breathless second and then fell.

The bowling center erupted in joyous bedlam. Tony's family and friends ran onto the lane and smothered his face with kisses, pounding him on the back.

As tears of happiness trickled down his face, Tony looked at the spectators. Behind them, he saw Papa's ghost proudly snapping his suspenders.

"See? I kept my promise," said Papa. He pointed to the gold medal pinned on his shirt and then he faded away.

Tony's mother sighed. "If only Papa were here to see this."

"He was, Mom. Papa was here."

Mom ruffled Tony's hair. "Of course, he was here in spirit. I know you had to be thinking of him while you bowled. But wouldn't it have been wonderful if he was *really* here to see you win?"

"Mom, I'm telling you, Papa was here!" Tony insisted. "I saw him!"

His mother smiled without saying anything more. Tony could tell she didn't believe him.

Sighing, Tony opened his bowling bag to put away his heavy ball when he noticed something rattling in the bottom of the bag. Puzzled, he reached in and pulled out a hard, flat, shiny object. It was his gold medal from the ABC Regionals—the very same one he had pinned on the shirt of his dead grandfather!

THE
PHANTOM TOUCH

Juwan Ellard had no idea he would get into the game. The wiry third-string quarterback accepted his role as a benchwarmer for Grandview High. Coach Ken Newman had even told him, "Juwan, I don't use sophomores at quarterback. You have a great arm, but you need a year to learn our complicated offense before I'll let you play."

So Juwan stood on the sidelines and watched his team, the Trojans, get whipped. Their defense was solid, but their offense seemed stuck in reverse, losing by scores of 12–0, 17–3, 21–6, and 14–7.

In their fifth game, the Trojans had only 44 total yards by the third quarter and trailed Oxford High 14–0. The mood of Coach Newman was darker than the chilly night. He was so fed up with the performances of his first- and second-string quarterbacks that he shouted to Juwan, "Ellard, warm up. You're going in the game when we get the ball back."

Juwan stood frozen, not believing what he had heard. Pointing to himself, he croaked, "Me?"

"Is there another Ellard on this team that I don't know about?" thundered the coach. "Yes, you! Warm up!"

Shaking with nervousness, Juwan picked up a football and began to loosen up. *This is my big chance to show everyone how good I am,* he thought. *A sophomore quarterback playing in a varsity game! Awesome!*

Moments later, his stomach churning with anxiety, Juwan charged out to the huddle and called the running play that Coach Newman had ordered. Juwan handed off to the fullback for a three-yard gain.

But then the referee blew the whistle. "Where's your mouthguard?" the ref asked Juwan.

Juwan stuck his fingers in his mouth and realized he wasn't wearing one. "It must have fallen out when I was on the sidelines. Why?"

"The rules say you can't play without a mouthguard. You'll have to go back to the bench. You can return once you find it."

Embarrassed and angry that he had wrecked his golden opportunity, Juwan scurried to the sidelines and sheepishly told his coach what had happened.

"For crying out loud, Juwan," growled Coach Newman. "Go find the darn thing." The coach called a timeout and ordered the players on the sideline to search under the bench, around the equipment, and in the grass. But no one could find the mouthguard in the shadows of the stadium lights. An irked Coach Newman had to put in the quarterback Juwan had replaced.

Juwan stomped away from the bench and threw his helmet down in disgust. What rotten luck!

Just then, he felt a sting on the back of his right calf. It was as if someone had pinched him on the bare skin between his sock and his pants. "Ouch!" Juwan yelped.

He looked down but couldn't see what had caused the prick.

As he was about to turn away, he spotted an object in the grass behind his right heel. He reached down and picked it up. It was his mouthguard! "Hey, Coach!" Juwan shouted, waving it in the air. "I found it!"

"Well, it's about time. Hang on to it this time. I'll put you back in on the next series."

If I hadn't been stung by something, I never would have found it, thought Juwan, jamming the mouthguard into his teeth. Minutes later, under his leadership, the Trojans began to click on offense. They marched down the field, scoring a touchdown in six plays. The TD pumped up the defense, forcing Oxford High to punt after three running plays netted only six yards.

On the Trojans' next drive, Juwan fired a twenty-three-yard touchdown pass. The point-after kick tied the game at 14–14, turning the usually quiet Grandview fans into cheering maniacs. In the fourth quarter, Juwan engineered another scoring drive. His fourteen-yard TD pass to fellow sophomore Andre Grissom capped a thrilling come-from-behind 21–14 victory.

In the joyous locker room after the game, Juwan's father arrived and heartily threw his arm around the young star's neck. "Congratulations, son! I almost jumped down from the stands to help you find your mouthguard."

"It's weird, Dad. The whole team and I had looked everywhere but couldn't find it. Then I felt a pinch on my leg. I looked down and there it was right at my foot."

"Who pinched you?"

Juwan shook his head. "No one was near me and it's

too cold for bugs to be out biting people. I don't know what caused it."

"Fate works in mysterious ways, son."

After he had dressed, Juwan proudly walked out of the locker room. He stood at the entrance to the gridiron and gazed at the scene of his greatest moment as an athlete. In the now empty Baker Stadium, he replayed each scoring drive in his mind.

I need a souvenir of this night, Juwan thought. He picked up an empty cardboard box and ambled to the middle of the field. At the fifty-yard line, he pulled out the pocketknife he always carried. Then he carved out a foot-square (.3-m) chunk of turf and placed it in the box.

Juwan was still kneeling when he felt someone patting him on the back. He smiled as he stood up, wondering who was congratulating him. But when Juwan turned around, he saw no one. *That's really strange,* he thought. *Am I still so happy about winning the game that I'm imagining someone patting me on the back?*

Juwan took the piece of turf home to the family's apartment in the public housing development a few blocks from the stadium.

The next morning, he looked for a place to transplant the sod. Unfortunately, there wasn't much in the way of grass. The area between his five-story apartment building and its twin was nothing but graffiti-marred cement. Bordering the cement were a dozen squares of dirt about two feet by two feet (.6 m x .6 m), where scraggly trees tried to survive city smog, too little sunlight, and pocketknife-wielding kids. Juwan placed the turf in one of the patches of dirt and carefully watered it with a borrowed sprinkler. He planned to do all he could to help the patch of turf survive.

At practice Monday, Coach Newman named Juwan the starting quarterback for the next Friday night's home game against the Reynolds High Rockets. Juwan worked hard during practice, throwing pinpoint passes to his wide receivers, including Andre, the fastest player on the Trojans.

Andre wasn't just the fastest, he was also the cockiest. "You and I are the only sophomores on the starting team, Juwan," he said, "but we'll shine like college stars on Friday." Pointing to his jersey, he added, "Just keep looking for number 88. I'll find a way to get open."

Before the game, Juwan sat quietly in front of his locker, going over plays that he had practiced throughout the week. Andre plopped down on the bench next to Juwan and remarked, "You don't seem your usual gung-ho self. Scared?"

"Nope, just thinking about the game."

"Don't think, man. Just throw it to number 88."

Juwan smiled. Then he felt someone hit him lightly on both shoulder pads. When Juwan looked up, Andre had a quizzical look on his face.

"Did you just tap me on the shoulder pads, Andre?"

"No, man. Did you do that to me?"

"Uh-uh."

Andre looked to the left, to the right, and behind him. Then he gazed at the ceiling before checking his shoulder pads. "You don't suppose some rats fell down from the overhead pipes and landed on us, do you? This old stadium is full of them. They're disgusting."

"I don't think it was rats, Andre. But I definitely felt something hit my pads." Juwan poked him in the ribs and added, "Maybe it was a phantom fan."

"Yeah, right, like there really could be one."

In the first half of the game, Juwan and Andre teamed up on two long touchdown passes, one for thirty-three yards and another for forty-two yards. Juwan also fired a quick slant-in pass to another receiver for a third TD, giving the Trojans a 21–3 lead over Reynolds.

When the Grandview players entered the locker room at halftime, they whooped it up and felt confident they would earn their second straight win.

"Listen up, men," Coach Newman ordered. "You played great out there. But we have another half to go. Reynolds is a good football team. They'll definitely play better in the second half—so we have to play better too."

Several times while the coach talked, he seemed bothered by an unseen annoyance and kept brushing the top of his right shoulder. "Linemen, I need you to do a better job of protecting the pocket for Ellard . . ." He stopped and rubbed his shoulder. "What the heck is going on? I must have a muscle spasm in my shoulder. Okay, now for you defensive backs . . ."

After Coach Newman finished his chalk talk, he walked over to Juwan and Andre. "Expect double coverage on Andre," said the coach, holding his shoulder and rotating his arm.

"We understand, Coach," said Juwan. "What's wrong with your shoulder?"

"I don't know. I feel this tapping sensation on my shoulder and I can't seem to get rid of it."

"The same thing happened—" Andre was interrupted by the referee, who opened the locker room door and shouted, "Kickoff in five minutes, Coach."

"Thanks," replied Coach Newman. Raising his voice, he barked, "Okay, men! Do what you did in the first half, only better! Let's go!"

As the coach predicted, the Rockets played much tougher in the second half. They struck for two quick touchdowns but missed both extra-point attempts. Juwan's offense sputtered and managed only a field goal. At the end of the third quarter, Grandview led 24–15.

In the fourth, Reynolds took advantage of a Trojan fumble and interception and scored two more TDs to vault ahead 29–24. Meanwhile, the Rockets' defense stopped the Trojans cold.

In the final minute, Juwan's desperation passes moved the ball to Reynolds's forty-one-yard line before the Trojans signaled for their final timeout with only five seconds left in the game. On the sideline, Coach Newman called for four receivers to run deep.

When Juwan returned to the huddle with the play, Andre declared, "Just throw the ball to me, Juwan. I'll do the rest."

The fans were on their feet as Juwan brought his team to the line of scrimmage. Andre was split far out to the left. The Rockets put seven defensive backs on the field—all positioned deep to prevent the long scoring pass.

On the do-or-die play, Andre raced down the left sideline and cut to the middle of the field. Juwan avoided the rush, stepped up in the pocket, and heaved the ball downfield just as Andre broke free from his defenders at the goal line. When Andre turned around, the ball was spiraling straight to him. *Here it comes—right into my hands!* thought Andre. The perfectly thrown ball landed on his fingers—and slipped right through them.

"Oh, nooooooooo!" wailed Andre, slumping to the ground as the ball bounced crazily in the end zone. On his knees, Andre pounded the turf and burst out crying. "I lost the game! I had it right in my hands!"

Juwan and several other teammates tried to comfort Andre, but it was no use. Finally, Juwan helped him to his feet and the two trudged into the locker room. Andre peeled off his uniform, refusing to talk to anyone. He kept his head down, too ashamed to make eye contact with his teammates. After almost everyone had left, he took a quick shower and dressed.

"Are you okay?" Juwan asked him.

"I honestly don't know. This is the worst thing that has ever happened to me. I dropped the bomb that would've won the game. How can I face my teammates? How can I face the school? My name will be mud on Monday."

"But, Andre, you caught two touchdown passes."

"No one is going to remember that. They'll remember that I dropped the winning TD pass. I just need to be alone. Tell my mama I'll walk home."

"I will. I'll call you tomorrow. Take care."

Andre left through the runway that took players onto the field. The grounds crew had finished picking up the trash and the lights had been turned off. Andre walked slowly over to the spot where he had dropped the ball. He sat down, rested his head on his raised knees, and sobbed.

That's when he felt an arm wrap ever so gently around

his shoulders and give him a comforting hug. *Coach Newman? Juwan? Mama?* he wondered. Andre lifted his head and was shocked to see that he was still very much alone. Fear flashed through him. He scooted back a few yards before jumping to his feet and rubbing his forearms.

I didn't imagine this. I felt an arm. Just like I felt someone tapping on my shoulder pad before the game. He shuddered and raced off the field.

The next morning, Andre walked over to Juwan's apartment building. Juwan was standing outside with a sprinkling can, watering the patch of dirt that contained the piece of turf from Baker Stadium.

"Andre, how are you feeling?"

"Lousy, man. Real lousy." Andre looked Juwan square in the eye. "Juwan, I promise that Grandview will never lose another game because of me dropping a pass. You'll still throw to me, won't you?"

"Andre, you're my main man. If I don't see you in the clear, it'll only be because I'm getting buried by a big bad lineman."

Andre pointed to the can. "What are you doing?"

"I'm watering my turf."

"Say what?"

"Promise you won't tell anyone."

"I'm cool, Juwan."

"After our win against Oxford, I went out to the middle of the field and carved out a chunk of grass to keep as a reminder of the game."

"You're strange, Juwan."

"Speaking of strange, after I dug it up, I felt a pat on the back. I turned around and no one was there."

"You know what, Juwan? After last night's game, I walked over to the goal line and I was cry—uh . . . thinking. Suddenly I felt someone put an arm around me. But I was all alone. It gave me the heebie-jeebies."

"Andre, something very bizarre is going on at the stadium. Before the game, we both felt tapping on our shoulder pads and we never figured out what it was."

"And at halftime, it looked like Coach Newman was getting tapped on the shoulder by an invisible I-don't-know-what."

Juwan snapped his fingers. "I just thought of something. After I couldn't find my mouthguard in the Oxford game, I felt a pinch on my leg. I looked down and there was my mouthguard lying in the grass. I don't know who or what pinched me."

"Do you think a ghost is haunting Baker Stadium?"

"I was joking when I mentioned the phantom fan. But maybe it's not such a joke after all."

They cut short their conversation when Mrs. Rose Watson, Grandview's short, gray-haired English teacher, walked past them. Mrs. Watson's husband Bill—whom everyone called Touch—had once been a star football player at Grandview. He earned a college football scholarship but a severe knee injury in his first collegiate game ended his playing days. He eventually became the Grandview football coach and had worked his way up to the position of the school's athletic director at the time of his death.

"Hello, boys," greeted Mrs. Watson. "I was at the game last night. Sure was exciting. Your team fought hard and you both made some great plays. You should have won."

Andre flinched. "I know. I dropped the winning pass."

"Oh, child, don't fret. Touch always said, 'Fame and shame are part of the game.'"

"I'm ready for the fame because I've felt the shame," Andre replied. "I know what I did wrong. I caught the pass before I caught it. You know what I mean? It seemed like a sure thing, so I didn't concentrate. I'll never let that happen again."

"Now that's something Touch would have liked to hear," said Mrs. Watson. "I sure do miss him. We would've been married forty-two years come December. But his old ticker gave out right before school started."

"We wish we could've met him," said Juwan.

"Well, you probably have met him—in an odd sort of way."

"Huh?" the boys asked in unison.

"Not too many people know this, but I guess it doesn't matter now," she said. "There's nothing anybody can do anyway."

"We aren't following you, Mrs. Watson," said Juwan.

"Touch loved football almost as much as he loved me. He was a terrific fullback. He held Grandview High's rushing and scoring records. Touch also played linebacker on defense and still holds the school record for the most tackles in a game.

"When Touch died, I had him cremated. I kept his ashes in an urn in the living room because I wanted time to think about what I should do with them. One day, I was going through his things when I came across a key to a gate at Baker Stadium—the place where he enjoyed his greatest glory as a football player.

"So I got this wonderful idea. One night, I took his urn to the stadium. I opened the gate and walked all around the field, scattering his ashes as I went. So you see, boys, Touch has been there on the field with you."

The boys looked wide-eyed at each other and then at the turf Juwan had been watering.

Seeing the sprinkling can, Mrs. Watson asked, "What are you watering, Juwan?"

Before he could answer, Andre changed the subject by asking, "How did your husband get the name Touch?"

"My husband had a thing about touching people. He liked physical contact—shaking your hand, patting your back, giving you a hug. But he had this silly superstition. He believed that if anyone touched him, he had to touch that person back. He simply wouldn't let anyone touch him last."

She broke into a chuckle. "His Grandview teammates found out about his superstition and nearly drove him crazy. One time, a player touched him with a football and then threw it over the fence at Baker Stadium. Touch jumped the fence and hunted for the ball until he found it. Once, his teammates ganged up on him, and they all touched him at the same time. Then they took off in different directions. What a hoot! He went crazy trying to touch them all back."

Mrs. Watson smiled at the memories. "Well, boys, it's been nice chatting with you, but I must get going or I'll be late for my tutoring lesson," she said.

As she walked off, Juwan grabbed Andre's arm and gasped, "Did you hear what she said? Do you think Touch's ghost is haunting the stadium?"

"It has to be, Juwan. But why now?"

"Maybe she has the answer."

The boys hurried to catch up with their teacher. "Mrs. Watson," Juwan asked, "exactly when did you spread your husband's ashes on the field?"

"The Thursday before last. I know that for a fact, because the next night you boys won your first game. I truly believe Touch brought you good luck."

"Yes," said Juwan, "his spirit has definitely touched us."

Added Andre, "More than you'll ever know."

The Cursed Glove

Angel Ruiz picked up a pebble on the infield dirt. No way did he want that little stone to cause a bad hop on a grounder, especially in the situation he was in now. With one out and the score tied late in the park league season opener, the Mavericks had runners on first and third.

The small but scrappy twelve-year-old shortstop for the Lopez Hardware Lizards put his glove near his face, turned to second baseman Luis Salazar, and whispered, "Cheat a little toward the bag. This batter is a pull hitter, so he probably won't hit to you. I want you ready to cover second in case the ball comes to me."

Luis nodded and moved several steps to his right. Meanwhile, Angel crouched low, poised like a cat ready to pounce. He tugged at his jersey, which overwhelmed his small and slender frame. In fact, the shirt was so big that parts of the L and the S in the name Lizards, stitched across the chest, were stuffed under his belt. The same was true for the number 10 on his back. But Angel didn't care. He'd play baseball in his underwear if he had to.

Anticipating where the ball might be hit, Angel inched

a few steps to his right moments before the Mavericks' Danny Dawson drilled a sharp grounder that skipped off the infield grass between short and third. The ball looked like it was headed into left field for a run-producing single.

But Angel dove to his right. While on his belly, he stretched out his left hand and snared the ball in the webbing of his glove with a sensational backhand stab. Scrambling to his knees, he fired a perfect throw to his teammate. Luis stepped on the bag at second, then pivoted and pegged the ball to first a split second before Danny crossed the base. It was a picture-perfect double play!

Angel dusted off his uniform and hustled over to the dugout, where his teammates pounded him on the back for making another great play. The beaming fielder kissed his glove and added, "I owe it all to my best friend Cucharon." He had named his glove after the Spanish word for "big scoop."

"It's the last inning," he told his teammates. "One run wins it for us. Let's get it!"

Angel soon came to bat with runners on second and third and two outs. A hit of any kind would win the game. As the rooting of his fellow Lizards rang in his ears, an overly eager Angel swung hard on the first pitch. The ball rose lazily in the air near second base, bringing groans from his teammates. Angry at himself over popping up, Angel slammed his bat down in disgust.

Surrounded by yells of "Drop it!" coming from the Lizards' dugout, the second baseman camped under the ball. It landed neatly in his glove—and then plopped out onto the dirt.

"He dropped it! He dropped it! We win! We win!" the Lizards screamed.

Angel happily jumped on first base and then joined his teammates in celebrating the victory. But Angel's joy was moderated when he noticed the look of utter sadness and humiliation on the face of the Mavericks' second baseman.

I feel sorry for him, Angel thought. *What a shameful way to lose a game. He must feel terrible.* Then he saw a hulking man in a white T-shirt and jeans lean over the boy. Although Angel couldn't hear what the man was saying, it was obvious he was chewing out the poor kid. *It must be his father. That's not right.* Angel trotted over to the boy, who was now standing alone, tears trickling down his cheeks.

"Don't let it get you down," said Angel. "Those things happen."

"I had it right in my glove," whimpered the boy, pounding his fist into his mitt.

"Yeah, I know. But I have to share some of the blame."

"How do you figure?"

"You wouldn't have been the goat if I had hit the ball harder. Hey, hang in there."

Angel lived and breathed baseball. He was one of those rare players who loved fielding more than batting. He was a decent batter—a singles hitter rather than a slugger—but an exceptional fielder.

His fondness for fielding came from his father, Roberto. While growing up in the Dominican Republic, Roberto was too poor to own a baseball glove or even shoes. But that didn't stop him from playing. He rummaged around in the trash and found an old milk carton. He cut it into the shape of a glove and tied it to his hand with pieces of string. Roberto—and many others like him—played baseball barefoot on rocky fields with makeshift gloves. One of those kids who used a milk carton for a mitt was Tony Fernandez, who grew up to become a major league All-Star.

Angel wanted to be a great fielder just like Fernandez, his favorite player. When Angel was six, he began bouncing a rubber ball against the wall of the service station where his father worked. Angel made a mark on the wall and practiced for hours throwing the ball at the spot. To improve his quickness and throwing accuracy, sometimes he would turn his back to the wall, then whirl and throw at the spot. He also threw the ball at the back steps of the service station and tried to anticipate which way the ball would carom.

Over the years, Angel developed an uncanny knack of knowing where to position his glove. At night, he often stood on the sidewalk and threw the ball as high as he could into the darkness and then tried to catch it when it came down through the glow of the streetlights.

Angel played with ratty, hand-me-down gloves that were usually too small or too big. But when he was nine, he received his very own new leather infielder's glove for Christmas. Because his parents could barely afford the glove, it was the only present he received from them that year. But it was the best present ever.

"It might be too big for you now, but your fingers will grow into it over time," Roberto told him. "This glove must last you a long, long time."

Holding the mitt in his hands for the first time, Angel tingled when he caressed the stitching and smelled the hide. For days afterward, he oiled the glove and worked the leather to form the perfect pocket. At first, he stuffed paper into the ends of the glove's fingers so it fit his hand better. After work, Roberto would hit him balls in the park until Angel could catch almost anything with that glove.

It was during one of those times with his dad that Angel unwittingly came up with the name for his glove.

"That's the way to scoop up the short hop," praised Roberto after Angel fielded a tough grounder.

Patting his glove, Angel said, "This is my Big Scoop, my Cucharon." The name stuck. And so did his habit of sleeping with his fingers snuggled inside his prized mitt.

By the time he was eleven, Angel was the best shortstop in the park league, fielding his position like a human vacuum cleaner. After his more spectacular plays, he always gave his Cucharon a kiss.

By anchoring the infield, Angel helped lead the Lizards to the league championship. The following year, the Lizards were the team to beat. But they got off to a shaky start by winning their opening game only because of the last-inning error by the Mavericks' second baseman.

For their next game, Angel and his teammates were pumped up and determined to play much better. But their mood turned somber when a league official made an announcement to the players and fans.

"Before the singing of the national anthem, I ask you to join with me in a moment of silence as we honor one of our league players, Chuckie Darden, who died three days ago in a tragic car crash."

"Who's he?" Angel whispered to Luis.

"I heard he played for the Mavericks."

"Wow, that's scary to think that somebody we played against just a few days ago is dead."

"Yeah. Let's not talk about it."

Once the game got underway, Angel and the Lizards focused on baseball and trounced the Chargers, 9–2.

That evening, the Ruiz family relaxed on the back porch of their house, celebrating the fifth birthday of Angel's brother Miguel. When their dog showed up in their yard, Angel announced, "Zorro is home. Hey, look. He's got something in his mouth."

"Not another dead squirrel, I hope," said his mother.

The big black dog often roamed far from the neighborhood. He was always bringing items home— usually gross things that no one wanted to touch.

In the darkness, Angel warily reached into Zorro's mouth, pulled out the object with two fingers, and then quickly tossed it toward his mother, Maria, warning, "Look out, Mama! It's a rat!"

Maria leaped off the chair with a shriek and hid behind Roberto. Then everyone but her burst out laughing. The object wasn't an animal at all. It was a baseball mitt. "Angel, you little devil!" said Maria. "You nearly turned my black hair white from fright."

"Sorry, Mama," said Angel, trying to keep a straight face.

He picked up the glove. It was a right-handed infielder's mitt that had hardly been used. "It looks like Zorro brought Miguel a birthday present."

"Whose glove is it?" asked Maria.

"I don't know, Mama. There's no name, only this mark." He pointed to the wrist strap, where someone had inked this symbol: ⚭

"Well, we can't keep it," claimed Maria. "It's an expensive glove that someone lost. Let's ask around the neighborhood. But don't tell anyone about the mark. That way, we'll be pretty sure that the person who can describe it is the real owner."

Despite talking to friends and neighbors and tacking up a sign at the ballpark, the family never found the owner. Meanwhile, the glove remained in Angel's messy closet.

Midway through the season, the first-place Lizards faced their arch rivals, the second-place Tigers.

In the fifth inning, with the score tied 4–4 and two outs, the Tigers loaded the bases. The batter hit a pop fly into shallow left field that the Lizards' third baseman lost in the sun. The left fielder, who had been playing more toward center, didn't have a prayer of reaching the ball. It looked like it would fall safely for a two-run double. But Angel, racing at full speed, made a lunging one-handed grab near the foul line to end the threat.

In the last inning, the Lizards were protecting a 5–4 lead. The Tigers had runners on first and third, but they were down to their last out. Jeff Cooper, the Tigers' best hitter, blasted a shot up the middle.

Angel dashed to his left, stretched as far as he could, and snagged the hot grounder. His momentum wouldn't let him stop to throw the ball, so he dove for second base. He slapped his glove on the bag just as the runner from first slid into second.

"You're out!" shouted the umpire.

Angel leaped to his feet and shouted, "We win! We win!" The Lizards threw their gloves in the air and celebrated in the center of the diamond.

"Angel, that glove of yours saved the day for us," marveled the coach. "I swear there's iron in the ball and a magnet in your glove."

"I love Cucharon. I'd be lost without it, Coach. Sometimes I think it doesn't even need me to hold it. It's magical."

Angel's smile quickly faded when he turned to pick up his mitt. His cherished glove was gone. "Has anyone seen Cucharon?" he asked, trying hard to stay calm. "Come on, which one of you wiseacres has my glove?"

His teammates shook their heads. None of them had it, and soon all of them were scouring the field in search of it. Meanwhile, a frantic Angel dashed over to the Tigers' side of the field.

"Did someone take my glove by mistake?" he asked.

"We don't have your stinking mitt," snarled Jeff Cooper.

Upset over his missing glove, Angel snapped back, "I think maybe one of you took it. You were probably sore at me because you lost."

"Don't flatter yourself. You didn't win the game by yourself. You're on a team," Jeff reminded him.

That night, Angel felt as though he had lost his best friend. "What am I going to do, Dad? I'm lost without Cucharon."

"What about the glove that Zorro brought home? It's an infielder's mitt, and it's practically brand-new."

"I don't want another glove. I want Cucharon!" Angel stormed off to his room and slammed the door.

After letting Angel cool off, Roberto went into his son's room and retrieved the glove from the closet. "Angel, maybe your glove will show up, maybe it won't. Why don't you use this one in the meantime? You know how tight money is. We simply can't afford to buy you a new one." Roberto flipped the glove in the air and added, "Maybe it was meant to be. Maybe Zorro found this fine mitt so you'd never be without one."

Angel halfheartedly grabbed the glove and slipped it on his left hand. "It's stiff."

"So oil it like you did with Cucharon."

"It doesn't feel right."

"Give it time. Work with it. A glove is only as good as the player who wears it." Seeing Angel pout, Roberto said sternly, "Look, it's either use this glove or give up baseball. Good night, Angel."

Angel flung the glove against the door and continued to stew. *If I ever find the jerk who stole Cucharon, I'll rip his eyeballs out and stuff them down his throat,* he thought.

After a while, Angel calmed down. He rolled off his bed and picked up the glove. Getting a ball from his closet, he lay back in bed, slipped on the glove, and began tossing the ball in the air and catching it with his mitt.

It feels so strange, he thought. *But it does have a good pocket and the webbing is strong. It definitely needs to be oiled. I'll try it out at practice tomorrow.* That night, he fell asleep with the glove on his hand.

"I've got it! I've got it!" yells the second baseman.

The ball rises in an arc and comes down between first and second base.

"Drop it!" come the shouts from the opponents' dugout as runners hustle toward third and home.

"It's mine!" yells the infielder. He looks up, holds his glove palm up, and watches the ball fall into the mitt—and then plop out onto the ground.

"He dropped it!" shouts a runner. "He dropped it! We win! We win!"

The shortstop walks up to the second baseman, flashes a look of disgust, and hisses, "You cost us the game, man! You blew it!"

"No, no, I didn't. I've got the ball right here . . ." Breathing heavily, Angel groped for the ball in his glove before he realized he was in his own bed. *Oh, good, it was only a bad dream. I never drop pop-ups.*

Angel looked at the glove on his hand. He took the mitt off and tossed it to the floor. Then he fell back to sleep.

The next day at practice, Angel hoped to hear that someone had returned Cucharon. But no one had. So he went ahead and practiced with the glove that Zorro had found. To Angel's relief, he fielded grounders nearly as well as he did with his old glove.

"It should be all right," he told Coach Marquez. "I need to break it in and get used to it."

Two days later, the Lizards played against the fourth-place Wildcats. Angel easily handled three routine plays with the new glove, but he struggled at the plate, striking out twice and grounding out once. None of the Lizards were batting well, yet they led 2–1 going into the last inning.

Jimmy Keller, the Lizards' best pitcher, retired the first two Wildcats. "One more out, baby!" shouted Angel. "One more and it's all over!"

On the next pitch, the batter hit a bouncer right to Angel. *Easy play*, he thought. The outfielders began to jog in from their positions because they were sure the game was about to end. Angel bent down to field the ball. But the ball bounced out of his glove and dribbled to his right.

"Oh, geez! No!" he groaned in horror. He quickly picked up the ball, but it was too late to make a throw. His ears turning red from embarrassment, Angel walked to the mound. "I'm sorry, Jimmy. I booted it."

"It's okay, Angel. I'll get this next guy out."

Unfortunately, the next batter clubbed one of Jimmy's fastballs over the center field fence for a game-winning two-run homer. The Lizards walked off the diamond in shock.

Fighting back tears, Angel threw the glove into the dugout and told his teammates, "I'm sorry, guys. If I had made the play on that easy grounder, we would've won. It was my fault."

"Don't blame yourself, Angel," said Coach Marquez. "We win as a team and we lose as a team. Errors are part of the game. Even the best players in the major leagues boot a ball now and then. Just forget about it."

But Angel couldn't. He hardly touched his dinner and went to his room to sulk. He lay in his bed with his ball and glove. *That never would've happened with Cucharon. Oh, sure, I've made errors before, but never when it cost us a game. I guess I'm not used to this glove.* Eventually, he fell asleep.

"What's the matter with you? Can't you do anything right? You are an embarrassment! What you did today makes me sick!"

From the shadows of a filthy kitchen emerges the bloated face of a wild-eyed man, bellowing at the top of his lungs. While he rants and raves, the drink in the glass he is holding spills onto the floor. Enraged, his hand crushes the glass, sending sharp slivers cascading onto his bare feet.

"Now see what you've done? Look how angry you've made me! Clean up this mess this instant!"

"I'm sorry!" Angel cried out. "I'm sorry!"

Roberto ran into his son's room. "Angel? What's wrong?"

Angel sleepily looked up at his father. "Dad, it's you. Oh, man, I must have been dreaming. Did I wake you?"

"You were yelling 'I'm sorry!'"

"It was a bad dream. A strange man was mad at me for something I had done, but I don't know what it was. I'm okay now."

Over the next few days, Angel took extra fielding practice, trying to get used to his glove and determined not to make another costly error.

Angel was itching to play when the Lizards faced the Bulldogs. In the second inning, he made a backhand stab on a sharp one-hopper, but he was unable to come up with the ball. Although the official scorer ruled it an infield hit, Angel was upset with himself. "I should have had that one," he told the coach when the inning was over.

In the fourth inning, Angel backpedaled as he tried to get under a shallow pop fly into left field. He reached back but the ball bounced off his glove. Angel quickly picked it up and fired to second, but the throw sailed over the second baseman's head, allowing the runner to reach third. Two batters later, the runner scored, giving the Bulldogs a 4–3 lead.

In the seventh inning, with the Lizards still on the short end of a 4–3 score, the Bulldogs had a runner on first and one out. The next batter hit a made-to-order double play grounder to shortstop. Angel bent down to scoop it up—and watched in disbelief as the ball scooted below his glove into left field. "Geez! What's happening to me?" He kicked the dirt and walked in a circle, trying to calm down. His error opened the floodgates, as the Bulldogs scored four more runs. The Lizards tried to mount a comeback but fell short, losing 8–6.

After the final out, Angel disgustedly flung his glove against the back wall of the dugout. "We've lost two straight games because of me and that no-good glove! I hate it!"

"Angel, the glove didn't cause that error," said Coach Marquez. "Not getting the glove down low enough to pick up the grounder did."

"I guess you're right."

"Is everything okay with you? You seem distracted."

"Everything is fine, Coach. Except . . . I'm not sleeping too well."

"Angel, I think you're worrying too much about this glove. Do you want to borrow someone else's?"

"No, I've got to get used to this one."

"You have shamed me, not to mention yourself!" *thunders the man with the bulging eyes and puffy face.*

He stalks to the closet, pulls out a baseball bat, and *holds it high as if he is going to beat someone. Instead, he* *bangs it hard on the kitchen table. "You and I are going out* *right now! Take your glove and get in the car!" He flings a* *baseball mitt that was on the table. In slow motion, the* *almost new infielder's mitt flips in the air. On the wrist strap* *is the symbol* ⊕.

Now he's in the car zooming down the street way over *the speed limit. "How many times have I told you? Keep* *your eye on the ball! Keep your eye on the . . ."*

The car starts to skid out of control on a curve. "Hold on *. . . I'm losing it . . . We're going to crash!" The windshield* *explodes as the car plows into a tree and rolls down an* *embankment. Then everything turns black.*

Angel bolted upright in bed, his breathing labored, his face drenched in sweat. "Why am I having these bad dreams?" he asked himself out loud. "Who is this man? What's happening? Was that my new glove in the dream?"

Angel didn't get any more sleep that night. The next morning, he walked sleepily into the living room, where his mother was watching the morning news on TV. Angel casually glanced at the television and froze. On the screen was a man in court, standing in front of a judge.

"That's him!" exclaimed Angel. "Mama, that's the man in my nightmares! Hurry, turn it up!"

On the TV, the reporter said, "Malcolm Darden pleaded guilty late yesterday afternoon to reckless homicide and drunken driving in connection with the death of his twelve-year-old son, Chuckie. On June 1, Darden was driving his car when he lost control and smashed into a tree. His son, who was in the front passenger's seat, was killed instantly, while Darden sustained minor injuries."

The camera then showed Darden standing in front of the judge, saying, "I am devastated by the loss of my son. I have no one to blame but myself. Chuckie was a good boy who loved baseball. His desire was greater than his talent, and I pushed him too hard. In the first game of the season, he dropped a pop-up that cost his team the game. I was angry and embarrassed, and in a drunken rage I ordered him into the car. I was taking him to the park to give him extra fielding practice when we crashed. . . ."

"Oh, my gosh!" Angel yelled.

"What is going on, Angel?"

"Mama, when did Zorro bring home the glove?"

"It was the fourth of June—your brother's birthday. Remember? We joked that Zorro had brought him a gift."

"This is too unreal."

"Angel, what are you talking about?"

Angel raced upstairs and returned moments later holding the glove. He pointed to the mark on the wrist strap. "Do you see this, Mama? This was Chuckie Darden's glove! Look. That's not a circle with a line down the middle. It's a C and a D joined together—Chuckie Darden's initials! Zorro must have found it at the crash scene a couple of days after the accident and brought it home. No one claimed the glove because Chuckie was dead and his father was in jail!"

Angel kept staring at the glove. "I didn't start getting those awful dreams until I began using his glove. Now I know where they came from. I was seeing things through Chuckie's eyes on the last day of his life!" He let the mitt drop from his hands. "Mama, this glove is cursed!"

Maria was so stunned she couldn't speak. Finally, she uttered, "That's the most unbelievable thing I've ever heard."

"But it's true. There's no other possible explanation."

"What are you going to do with the glove?"

"Give it back to the real owner."

"But how are you going to do that? He's dead."

Angel didn't answer. He ran outside and grabbed a trowel. Then he hopped on his bike, hooked the glove on the handlebars, and pedaled over to the cemetery.

After he found Chuckie's tombstone, Angel kneeled down in front of it and said, "I feel bad for you, Chuckie, because you didn't deserve to die so young. I'm sorry that things didn't go right for you during your last game. I know you tried your best. Here's your glove. It's a nice one, but I don't want it because it's caused me a lot of trouble."

Angel took out the trowel and dug a hole in front of the gravestone. Then he buried the glove. "I'm hoping those nightmares about you and your dad will end now," he said.

As Angel headed home, he wondered what he was going to do for a mitt. *I guess I can borrow Coach Marquez's old one. Maybe I can earn money doing odd jobs. But it'll take me forever to buy a new glove. Hey, is that Zorro? What's he got in his mouth?*

The dog, his head held high, trotted around the side of a house.

"Zorro! Come here, boy."

Just then Jeff Cooper, the slugger for the Tigers, ran out of the house, shouting, "Hey, you mangy mutt, get back here with that—" The boy skidded to a halt when he spotted Angel. Jeff then wheeled around and dashed back into his house.

"Here, Zorro," called Angel. Wagging his tail, Zorro pranced over to Angel and dropped the object that had been tenderly clutched between his jaws.

Angel picked it up and whooped for joy. "Cucharon!"

THE FIELD OF DEATH

Jenna Arnold raced down the right side of the soccer field. After dodging one defender and slipping past another, she cut to the middle and received a perfect pass from her teammate Erica Craven. Jenna had a clear shot at the net. She cocked her leg—and then tripped over a clod of dirt and tumbled to the ground.

"I hate this field!" Jenna fumed. "It's nothing but yucky dirt and bumps."

Coach Kay Roxbury blew her whistle. "Quit beefing," she ordered. "Yes, it's a terrible field, but it's only temporary until we move to the new field in a few weeks. In the meantime, I don't want to hear any more complaining."

It was the third day of practice for the girls' soccer team at the just-opened Munson Middle School, a state-of-the-art facility carved out of pastureland west of town. While workers installed the underground sprinkler system on the main field, the girls had to practice behind the school on a crude, lumpy dirt area. The girls didn't know it yet, but there was an unearthly secret right beneath their feet.

During soccer drills on the fourth day of practice, Jenna spotted a tall woman, whose face was shielded by an old-fashioned straw bonnet, strolling across the north end of the field. Her puffy white blouse flapped in the breeze, and her long red skirt brushed against her black high-button shoes.

"Who's that?" Jenna asked Erica.

"I've never seen her before. Maybe she's one of the drama students."

"I can't make out her face, but she looks like an adult."

The girls returned to their footwork drills. Moments later, when Jenna looked up, the woman was gone.

The following day at practice, the team was doing jumping jacks when Jenna once again saw the mysterious woman ambling across the field.

"Hey, Erica, look," said Jenna. "It's the bonnet lady. Let's see where she goes."

While following her with their eyes, the two girls didn't realize they had slowed down and were not in sync with the rest of the team.

"Erica! Jenna!" Coach Roxbury thundered. "Get over here. I will not have any slackers on this team!"

To everyone's surprise, including her own, Erica burst out crying. Seeing her best friend sobbing, Jenna began bawling too.

Coach Roxbury was mystified. "Girls, what's wrong with you two?"

"I . . . I don't know," blurted Erica. "You're so mean."

"I am not, Erica. I am the coach. The coach is supposed to bark at the players to motivate them."

"You didn't have to make us cry," whined Jenna.

Coach Roxbury threw up her hands. "What I said was no big deal. Come on, get over it. Don't be so sensitive."

The girls wiped their noses with the back of their hands and looked sheepishly at their teammates.

"Just out of curiosity," asked the coach, "what were you two looking at?"

"The lady in the bonnet," Jenna replied. "We were wondering who she was."

Coach Roxbury looked across the field. "I don't see anyone."

"She's not there now," said Jenna. "She was dressed like a prairie woman from a long time ago."

"We saw her yesterday at practice," Erica added.

"Look, girls, I'm counting on you two to be leaders on this team. Focus on soccer, not on prairie women. I need committed soccer players, not crybabies!"

Erica's bottom lip began to quiver and Jenna's eyes welled up with tears as they went back to their positions. With some effort, they managed to complete their team exercises without further emotional displays.

During a break later, Erica muttered to Jenna, "I could just kick myself for crying like that. I looked like a blubbering fool."

"Me too. You know me. I might cry in my room but not in front of others. It's not like Coach Roxbury said anything so awful to us."

"I know, Jenna. I can't explain it, but I just felt like crying."

The next day, the team engaged in a practice game that seemed to bring out the worst in everyone. The girls shoved, pushed, and banged into each other as if they were in an intense grudge match. They snarled and glared like arch rivals.

Halfway through the game, Jenna broke free in front of the net. But Dawn Farraday stuck her foot out, causing Jenna to trip and slam hard into the dirt. In a flash, Jenna leaped to her feet and pushed Dawn.

"You tripped me on purpose, you jerk!" Jenna snarled.

"I was going after the ball," Dawn protested.

"It was a deliberate foul."

"What are you going to do? Cry?"

With a yell, Jenna lunged at Dawn and tackled her. Coach Roxbury began blowing her whistle as the other girls tried to pull their fighting teammates apart. When Hallie Loman used a little extra force in prying free Jenna's arms, Erica grabbed Hallie around the waist and dragged her away. That caused Hallie's good friend Anna to jump on Erica's back. Seconds later, members of the entire team were screaming and wrestling on the field.

Coach Roxbury kept blowing her whistle until the veins in her neck looked like runaway hoses. "Stop it! Stop it!" she yelled until she was hoarse.

Finally the coach dove into the pile and began yanking girls away one at a time. At the bottom of the pile, Jenna and Dawn were still clawing at each other. Coach Roxbury grabbed them by the arms and pulled them to their feet. After seeing their scratched and dirt-smudged faces, the coach snapped, "You two should be ashamed of yourselves for your behavior. For that matter, all of you should. You acted so irresponsibly. No, worse than that. You acted like . . . boys!"

Only then did Coach Roxbury realize that the girls'

heaving shoulders weren't from heavy breathing, but from crying. Face after face was streaked with tears.

"What's wrong with you people? This is a soccer field, not a battlefield. We are a team, get it? If we war among ourselves, we can never expect to beat the other team. I like a spirited practice, but this is ridiculous. We must work together as a unit and show respect toward each other. If this were a real game, the referee would have red-carded the whole team. Practice is over—except for one thing."

"We know, a lap around the field," said Erica.

"No, five laps around the field. Now move!"

As the girls broke into a trot, Erica asked Jenna, "What happened to you out there? I thought you and Dawn were friends."

"I know, but she tripped me and I went ballistic. I can't figure out what's happening to me. First I cry in front of my teammates and now I start a brawl. If my parents find out, they'll say something stupid like maybe it's my hormones kicking in."

"But, Jenna, no one seemed to be herself today. I felt really on edge for no reason. When the fight started, I had the urge to twist Hallie's arms and pull Anna's hair. Actually," she whispered, "I did both—but not too hard."

"Erica, did you see the look in the other girls' eyes? They were out for blood. Hey, there she is again." Jenna pointed to the north end of the field. "It's the bonnet lady."

"She's wearing the same thing as before. Let's get a closer look." The girls picked up their pace, passing Dawn, Hallie, and the others. But by the time the two reached the other side of the field, the bonnet lady was nearing the remains of an old shack.

The one-room structure lay fifty yards beyond a rusted barbed-wire fence that separated the soccer field from a seldom-used pasture. The rotted roof and worm-eaten wood sides had collapsed long ago. Only a crumbling stone chimney stood defiantly against the ravages of time.

"How did she get to the other side of the barbed wire?" Jenna asked Erica.

"I don't know. I didn't see her climb over it. Maybe a section of the fence fell down."

Just then Dawn and Hallie dashed past them. "We can't let them get away with that," said Jenna. She broke into a faster sprint, with Erica at her heels. On the final lap, the four of them were bunched together, running full bore. Unfortunately, Dawn's right heel caught Erica's left foot, causing them to stumble into Hallie and Jenna. After a few seconds of awkward struggling to keep their balance, the four of them tumbled to the ground.

"You deliberately cut me off!" shouted Erica.

"You got too close!" retorted Dawn.

Before they could start another fight, Coach Roxbury stepped in and bellowed, "Sit down in the center of this field and don't leave until you've worked it out."

Minutes later, the four girls marched over to her. "We're sorry, Coach," Erica said. "Things got out of hand."

"We've apologized to each other," added Jenna.

"It won't happen again," said Hallie.

"It was a silly, stupid fight," Dawn agreed. "We just got caught up in the spirit of combat. Everything's cool now."

"Good," said the coach. "I don't want to see a repeat.

Play hard but fair. Look after your teammates. And save your competitive flair for the Conniston game next week."

Despite the team's promise to work together, squawking and bickering filled the air at the next practice. Although no fights broke out, their testy attitude baffled the coach. It would take another few days before she and the girls understood why.

Jenna's mother, Renee, and family friend Hope arrived at the end of practice to pick up Jenna and Erica. While walking off the field, the girls spotted the bonnet lady again, this time at the old shack. They saw her step behind the stone chimney, but she didn't reappear.

"Can you wait a few minutes, Mom?" asked Jenna. "I want to check out who this person is."

"I'll go with you, Jenna," said Hope. As they walked across the field, Hope told her, "I have a very odd feeling about that woman."

"Uh-oh, is this your psychic side talking?"

Hope nodded. She was a professional psychic who had her own local call-in radio show. On several occasions, she had worked with the police, using her psychic power to help them find clues to crimes.

Hope began to shiver and wrapped her hands around her forearms. "I'm getting bad psychic vibrations about this field, Jenna. It feels like . . ." She hesitated.

"Like what? Please tell me."

"Death. It feels like death."

They hurried across the field, gingerly stepped over the barbed-wire fence, and reached the remains of the shack. Jenna looked around. "There's no sign of the bonnet lady, Hope. She's gone."

"I'm not so sure," replied the psychic, her eyes closed and her hands spread out in front of her. "I can feel the presence of a woman, a very sad woman who lived a long time ago. I can't get a complete picture in my mind yet. There are too many people around. Let's go back."

"Could this woman be the bonnet lady?" asked Jenna.

Hope didn't say anything.

"Hope, you can tell me. I'm not a little kid anymore. You're the one who told me I have psychic gifts that need to be developed, remember? And you said Erica might be psychic too."

"You're right, Jenna." Hope stopped and squeezed the girl's hand. "I believe the bonnet lady is a ghost."

"A ghost? On a soccer field?" Jenna's eyes lit up with excitement. "That's totally awesome!"

"Who she is and why she's appeared I can't say," said Hope. "But I want to find out. Jenna, how long has the team been practicing on this field?"

"About a week."

"Has anyone used it before the soccer team?"

"No, this is a new school, so we're the first ones to practice here. It's only temporary."

"Think carefully, Jenna. Have you picked up any kind of psychic impressions on this field? Anything at all?"

"No, but I've been much more emotional. So has Erica. We both cried during practice earlier this week because the coach yelled at us. And I've felt angry for no reason. I even got into a fight. Actually, the whole team fought, and that's not like us. We all played soccer together at our old school, and we always got along. But lately we've been at each other's throats."

"Did any of these feelings exist on the team last year at the old school?"

Jenna shook her head. "Why are you asking me these questions?"

"Because contrary to what you think, your answers tell me that you are picking up psychic vibrations from this field." Holding her hands straight out, palms down, Hope declared, "I definitely feel death here, and I believe the bonnet lady is somehow connected. We're going to find out why."

Later that night, Hope returned to the field with Jenna, Renee, and Erica to conduct a seance. They sat on the ground in the center of the field, facing each other. They held hands and focused their thoughts on the bonnet lady.

Minutes later, peering into the darkness, Jenna blurted out in a hushed but excited tone, "Someone is coming toward us."

"It's her," Erica exclaimed in a loud whisper.

The bonnet lady stood still, about twenty feet away. It was light enough for them to see she was wearing the same clothes as before. But it was too dark to see the features of her face.

"We come as friends," Hope said softly. "We come to learn from you. Tell us why you roam this field. Tell us why I feel a sense of heartache and death."

In a frail voice, the bonnet lady spoke. "My name is Lizzy Mahoney. I am the wife of Michael Mahoney, a hardworking farmer and a decent man. We moved here in 1865 to work the land and build our house close to Fort Haywood, the army post. It has not been an easy life, but we were all thankful—my husband and I and our two boys, Conner and Casey." She began to weep. "Now, two years later, all that is precious to me is gone, like the meadowlarks in winter."

"Lizzy, tell us what happened," Hope gently urged.

"Cholera," answered Lizzy. "A horrible cholera epidemic struck the entire area. I volunteered to help the doctor. I'm not a trained nurse, but I tried to bring hope to the sick and comfort to the dying. I packed flannel cloths and hot bottles around the bodies of the patients to keep them warm. I gave them sips of barley water and beef tea. I held their hands.

"I hoped my family would be spared from this plague. I tried so hard to be careful, boiling utensils and burning the patients' contaminated clothes. But cholera is so contagious. Too many flies, too much bad water.

"My darling four-year-old Conner was the first to get sick. In only three days, he was dead. Casey suffered the same fate a week later. He had just turned six. I was losing my mind from grief when my beloved Michael fell ill. I tried so hard to save him, but I'm no match for a disease that strikes the strong as well as the weak. Michael held on for five days before he died.

"My whole family was gone, just like that. I wanted them all close to me, so I buried them here. I helped dig the graves myself."

"Did you bury them in this field, Lizzy?" Hope asked.

"Yes."

"But, Lizzy, there are no tombstones, no sign that this is a family cemetery."

"I had no money for fancy gravemarkers, so I used flat stones. But now I can't find them. I hear noise. I hear children, but they're not my sons. Where are the graves of my boys, of my husband? I must be with them. Help me . . . help me . . ."

Lizzy's voice faded away, and so did her ghost.

A minute of silence, broken only by the chirping of crickets, followed the spirit's extraordinary appearance.

"That was the most astounding experience I've ever had," Renee murmured. She looked over at her daughter, who was silently crying. "Jenna?"

"Mom, I feel so sad and weird—and scared."

"Me too," said Erica, burying her head in her hands.

After the girls had regained their composure, Renee asked Hope, "What does all this mean?"

"Lizzy has been making her presence felt because of an unresolved conflict. I'm guessing it's because the girls are playing soccer on what no one knew was sacred ground."

Jenna winced. "We're using Lizzy's family cemetery as a practice field?"

Erica jumped up. "Eeeewwww! We've been playing over the bodies of dead people!"

"Jenna and Erica are psychically sensitive girls," Hope explained. "That's why they've been so emotional whenever they step on this field. Obviously, other members of the team have been affected too."

"So what do we do now?" asked Renee.

"Ladies, it's time we start digging," Hope declared.

"Here?" the others gasped.

"No, at the county library. We need to check out Lizzy's story."

The next morning, the four arrived at the library and thumbed through historical accounts of the area. They learned that a cholera epidemic had swept through the county in 1867, killing more than one hundred people.

Further research showed that Michael Mahoney bought ten acres in 1865 that included the land where Munson Middle School was built. Part of the property was later sold off by the family's relatives.

"Somehow over the years the stones used as gravemarkers for Lizzy's family disappeared," Hope said. "They probably toppled over, and weeds grew over them. Distant relatives sold the land, and no one knew about the graves."

"We need to find those graves," said Jenna. "We can't play soccer on a family plot."

"That's true," Hope said. "Lizzy's ghost won't rest until the graves of her loved ones are no longer disturbed."

"But our first game of the season is next week—on our temporary field," Erica pointed out. "We can't let that happen."

"How are we going to find the graves?" asked Renee.

"We'll find them," Hope promised.

That evening, the four held another seance at the field, seeking the return of Lizzy's ghost. She didn't disappoint them.

"Lizzy, we can help you," said Hope, when the ghost appeared. "But you must help us first. Where exactly on this field is your family buried?"

Lizzy fretted, her head turning to the left and right. "I'm not sure," she answered. "Everything looks so different. The markers are gone. So are the lilac bushes and the two birch trees. I don't know. But they're here . . . they're here . . ." Lizzy then vanished into the darkness.

"We'll have to find the graves ourselves," Hope told the others.

"Whenever she's appeared, it's been on the north end of the field," said Jenna.

Added Erica, "And that's where all the fighting and other bad stuff has happened to our team."

Hope walked over to the north end and stretched her arms out in front of her. Then ever so slowly she walked back and forth, trying to detect any psychic vibrations. "Here," she said, pointing at her feet. "I feel that a child is buried here."

Renee stuck a pencil into the ground to mark the spot. Moments later, Hope marked two more places, all within twenty feet of each other.

"We found them!" said Erica.

"Wait," Hope said, her arms still extended. "I feel a psychic impression of a fourth grave. It's a woman's."

"Lizzy's?" asked Jenna.

They crowded at the spot where Hope was standing. Instantly, Jenna and Erica burst into tears.

"I feel so sad," Jenna sobbed.

"It's like I can feel her heartache," Erica said.

The next day, Hope convinced officials to dig up the graves at the spots she had marked. Four rotting pine boxes—two adult-sized and two smaller ones—were brought to the surface. So were four flat stones. The forces of nature had erased whatever names had been etched on the gravemarkers. However, there was no doubt whose remains were in the coffins.

Although the school board technically now owned the land, officials decided to rebury the remains in the same graves and fence off a section of the field as a cemetery. Erica and Jenna were thrilled. Lizzy Mahoney's spirit could finally rest in peace. Meanwhile, the team practiced on the front lawn of the school and arranged to play its game against Conniston at a different location. The following week, the new permanent field was ready for practice and games. The Munson Middle School girls' soccer team was once again a happy bunch of players—except, of course, when Coach Roxbury made them run laps after practice.

THE PEP TALK

Karim Rasheed walked aimlessly down the side street, his hands stuffed inside the pockets of his baggy pants. His left foot took a swipe at an empty soda can and sent it spinning against a utility pole.

Karim had been in Bellwood for less than a week, but he had made up his mind he wasn't going to like living here.

Why couldn't Mama stay in Decatur? the ten-year-old grumbled to himself. *I knew everybody there. I could be playing with my friends right now. But I'm stuck in this boring town because Mama wants to be near her kin. If only the factory hadn't closed. Then we wouldn't have moved and I wouldn't be starting a new school Monday and having to make all new friends.*

While the setting January sun gave way to twilight, Karim started toward home. But then he heard the faint sounds of squeaking shoes, a thumping ball, and shouting kids. *I wonder where the basketball game is?* he thought.

Karim enjoyed playing hoops. Although he was tall for his age, he was a so-so rebounder, mainly because he wasn't aggressive enough under the basket. It didn't help that he wasn't all that coordinated. And his outside shooting was the pits. But he still liked to play.

The sounds came from a weather-beaten abandoned warehouse across the street. The wood siding had faded and peeled, revealing several layers of old paint.

Karim tried to peek into the grimy windows, but they were too high. Strangely, he saw no light coming from inside. Even more odd, the front and back doors were padlocked and secured with a chain.

Karim pressed his ear against the back door. *Yeah, kids are playing basketball. How did they get in there if the doors are chained from the outside? There must be another entrance, but where? And how come there's no light inside?*

"Hey, you!" A gruff young voice behind him startled Karim. "What's up?"

Karim wheeled around and faced a boy his age—but bigger and more muscular—wearing a Chicago Bulls jacket and holding a basketball under his arm.

"Nothing much," said Karim. "I thought I heard kids playing hoops here and—"

"Inside this old building?" The boy grinned. "Man, you're hearing things. It's empty. Been that way for years."

"Come over here and listen for yourself," said Karim.

The boy warily walked over. "I don't hear anything."

Surprised, Karim put his ear to the door. But this time he heard none of the sounds. "Well, I heard the kids earlier. And the noise came from inside."

"Yeah, right." The boy smiled mockingly and then fired the basketball at Karim. "Think fast!"

Karim managed to get his hands up just in time to keep

the ball from slamming into his face. He chased down the ball and threw it back as hard as he could. The bigger kid stuck out his right hand, tipped the ball into the air, and caught it with his left hand. "That's a sorry excuse for a throw," he sneered.

"I didn't throw it that hard," replied Karim. "I was being nice."

"You're not from around here, are you?"

"I am now. I moved into the neighborhood this week. My name is Karim."

"I'm Billy Ray. But my friends call me Hacker." The bigger kid sized up Karim. "Do you play hoops?"

Karim nodded.

"Are you any good?"

Karim shrugged.

"That bad, huh? There's an outdoor court on Third Avenue and Seventh Street two blocks from here. We play hoops most every day. Come by after school—then maybe you'll see why they call me Hacker." Hacker started to walk off, then stopped. "Oh, and the sounds of kids playing hoops will be real—not imaginary," he said with a chuckle.

The next day, Karim went to Third Avenue and Seventh Street, expecting to find other boys his age playing basketball. Instead, he saw a construction crew chopping up concrete. Hacker and five other boys were raising their fists and yelling at the workers.

"What's going on, Hacker?" Karim asked.

"They're taking away our court," fumed Hacker. "The city says they need the space for an outreach center supposedly to help us kids. So they wipe out our only fun.

It's bogus!" Hacker flung his basketball against a chain-link fence in disgust. "Now where are we going to play?"

"What about the empty building?" Karim suggested.

Hacker looked at the other kids. "That's not such a bad idea. My uncle George knows the owner. Maybe he can work something out."

The following day, Karim joined Hacker and several boys and adults, including George, at the warehouse. "This building has a checkered past," said George. "It's been everything from a dance hall to a practice gym to a warehouse for furniture, cotton, and textbooks." George unlocked the door and let everyone inside.

The warehouse was one large area with exposed wooden rafters in the ceiling. At one end, cardboard and packing material had been piled on top of small machinery. The rays of the sun struggled to pass through the grime-covered windows, casting a dull, hazy light onto the filthy wood floors. Each step the visitors took kicked up dust.

No one has been in here for a long while, thought Karim. *There's no way anyone played basketball in here the other night.*

"This could make a great youth center," said George. "It's long enough for full court basketball. We'll need to clean it up, sand the floors, and put in lights. And I'm sure the wiring has to be replaced—the electricity's been turned off for years."

Over the next week, the neighborhood boys chipped in to help spruce up the place. George brought in two used hoops with backboards and an old electric scoreboard donated by the state university.

While the boys waited for the warehouse to be rewired, they played basketball by the sunlight shining through the now-cleaned windows. Karim painfully learned why Billy Ray was known as Hacker. On defense, Billy Ray hacked and slapped the dribbler's hand. Under the boards, he elbowed and shoved opponents out of the way. He had bloodied the lip of everyone he played against—including Karim.

One day, after getting an elbow in the mouth, Karim rushed home to put ice on his fat lip. He quickly returned to the warehouse, but by then everyone had left and the place was locked. As he started to walk away, he again heard the muffled sounds of kids playing basketball.

How can they be playing hoops? It's getting too dark to see inside, Karim told himself. He propped an old crate against the side of the building and stood on it so he could gaze into the window.

Karim couldn't believe what he saw—absolutely nothing. Yet the sounds remained loud and clear. When he discovered the window wasn't locked, he opened it and slipped inside. As soon as his feet hit the floor, the sounds of the basketball game ceased.

"Hello? Is anybody here?" Karim called out. He had an uncanny feeling he wasn't alone. Someone was staring at him. He scanned the warehouse, but the twilight made it difficult to see inside. Every dark corner looked as if it hid a lurking figure. "Hello?"

Silently, from out of the shadows, a tall, broad-shouldered young man of about twenty stepped forward in the dim light. His muscular forearms bulged under a sleeveless white T-shirt. Clad in jeans and ankle-high black sneakers, he nodded and flashed a friendly smile, revealing a perfect set of teeth. Long eyebrows angled over his sleepy-looking eyes. A scar across his forehead marred his otherwise smooth, shaved, egg-shaped head.

"Hello there," he said in a low voice.

"Uh, hi," replied Karim. "I thought someone might be here."

"My name is Orlando Huckaby."

"I'm Karim Rasheed. Glad to meet you. Did you hear kids playing basketball just a moment ago?"

"I hear those sounds all the time in here. Did you know this warehouse was once used for practice by the high school basketball team? It was years ago, before the school had a gym. In the dead of winter, this place was like an icebox, heated only by a wood-burning stove. Bellwood High still had a super team in spite of being without a gym."

Karim's attention was snagged suddenly by a faint glow and a sputtering electrical noise. He turned around and was surprised to see the old scoreboard lit up. Although several bulbs were burned out, he could still read the score: VISITORS 45, HOME 44.

"How could the scoreboard be turned on?" Karim asked. "I thought there wasn't any electricity in the . . ." He stopped talking when he realized that Orlando had disappeared. "Orlando? Where are you? Hello?"

Karim walked to the corner where Orlando had first emerged, but Orlando wasn't there. Nor was he anywhere else in the warehouse. *This is nuts. How could he sneak out like that without me seeing him?* Karim thought. *For that matter, why would he even bother?*

Karim tried both the front and back doors, but they were still locked. *The window I came in is open. But if he went out there, he would've gone right past me.*

As Karim scratched his head in puzzlement, the scoreboard flickered twice and then went out. Thinking the electricity was working, Karim flipped a light switch. Nothing happened.

Starting to feel uncomfortable, Karim climbed out of the window and closed it. He was walking away when he once again heard the faint sounds of a basketball game.

If I tell anyone I saw the scoreboard go on by itself, they'll laugh at me. Karim thought. *The other boys already think I'm nuts because Hacker told them I heard invisible basketball players. I'd better keep my mouth shut.*

As promised, the wiring soon was finished and the electricity was turned on. The scoreboard worked fine once the burned-out bulbs were replaced. The basketball floor was sanded and painted with all the necessary lines and circles. New lights were installed. The youth center, headed by George, was finally ready for basketball.

Karim became a reserve on the youth center's team, the Falcons. George, the coach, set up games with centers in nearby towns. He believed that if you showed up for practice, you played—no matter how good or bad you were. So he gave reserves like Karim quality minutes in both halves.

In the season opener, played in the nearby town of Plainfield, the Falcons were trounced 48–29 by the Pitbulls. The Falcons then lost to the Chesnee Hornets 39–32. Karim played a total of eight minutes in the games, picked up four fouls, collected three rebounds, and missed all six shots from the field. Hacker scored forty of the Falcons' sixty-one points. But he also fouled out of both contests.

The Falcons were psyched for their next game—their first at home in the warehouse. Karim's mother and his aunts and uncles arrived, bringing their own folding chairs because the place had no bleachers.

"I'll score lots of points for you today, Mama," promised Karim.

The Falcons and the Goshen Jaguars battled to a 20–20 tie at the half. Karim, who was still looking for his first basket of the year, started the third quarter.

Inspired by the cheers of his family, Karim played with uncommon aggressiveness. He snared two rebounds, stole a pass, and knocked the ball away from a dribbler, leading to a mad scramble and a jump ball at midcourt.

The ball was tipped to Karim, who dribbled past one defender and headed down the lane for an easy layup. *Yes!* He beamed. *My first basket!*

Pumping his arms in happiness, he glanced at his mother and was perplexed because she wasn't clapping. Instead, she had a quizzical look on her face. He gazed at the rest of his relatives. They too weren't reacting the way he had expected.

Then one of the Jaguars slapped him on the back and said, "Thanks, man! Hope you score some more for us!"

"What?"

Hacker bounded over to Karim. "What's the matter with you, Karim? You just shot into the wrong basket and scored for the other team!"

Karim looked at George, who called time and motioned his players over to the bench. "Karim, did you forget that we change baskets after the half?" the coach asked.

"I know that. I just got confused. I'm sorry, George, really I am."

Karim slumped down on the bench, not daring to look at his family. But he couldn't help hear his mother say, "That's okay, honey. You're hustling and trying hard. Don't be discouraged. It's only two points, so it won't mean a thing."

Unfortunately, it did. Karim hoped that if the Falcons lost, it would be by more than two points. But as luck would have it, they lost by exactly two points, 37–35—and everyone knew who had scored the critical basket.

"We would've won the game if we hadn't made stupid mistakes," griped Hacker afterward. He used the word "we," but that didn't lessen the shame that stung Karim.

As players and family filtered out of the youth center, Karim's mother put her arm around her teary-eyed son and tried to comfort him. "Look at the bright side, sweetie. You scored your first basket of the year."

Karim rolled his eyes. "Mama, I'm going to stay here in the gym for a while. I'll meet you at home later."

He picked up a basketball and began shooting jumpers, one after the other, until everyone had left except for George. "Karim, I'm leaving now," the coach told him.

"I'd like to stay."

"Okay, but make sure you turn off the lights and lock the door when you leave."

Karim continued to shoot baskets—missing most of them but still trying. After swishing two jumpers in a row, he heard someone clap. "Orlando," Karim said. "How long have you been here?"

"Long enough to see you're hurting."

"Yeah, I scored the winning basket for the other team. I've embarrassed my family, my teammates, and especially myself."

"No matter how bad things may seem now, in the scheme of things, it's no big deal," said Orlando. "How many people do you suppose live in New York City?"

"What's that got to do with basketball?"

"I'll tell you. There are over eight million. How many do you think know what happened to you today?"

"None."

"How many people in Mexico City, Paris, London, and Moscow know what happened to you?"

"None."

"And here in Bellwood?"

"Everyone."

"No, only the few people who were at the game. That's it. And they'll soon forget. You won't have newspaper reporters asking you questions. You won't have the coach saying how disappointed he was in you. You won't have fans hounding you. No, what happened today is nothing more than proof that you are human and not perfect. Don't let it get you down. Keep plugging away. If you don't find success here, you find it somewhere else. Your worth as a person is not judged on how well you perform on the basketball court."

With a buzz, the scoreboard unexpectedly lit up. But it didn't give the score of the Falcons–Jaguars game. Instead it read: VISITORS 45, HOME 44, just as it had the other day.

Karim walked over to the scorer's table and noticed that the switch on the control panel was in the "off" position. He tapped it and the scoreboard lights went blank.

"That's the weirdest thing, isn't it?" Karim said. He looked up from the table. Orlando was gone. *How does he do that? I didn't hear the door open or close.*

Suddenly there was a knock at the door. "Hello?" called a woman standing outside. "Is anyone inside?"

Karim went to the door and opened it. A gray-haired woman smiled at him. "I heard the youth center was looking for donations of sporting goods," she said. "I have lots of things in my car, and they aren't doing me any good. I'm not exactly the athletic type," she added with a giggle. "Do you mind carrying them in for me?"

"Certainly not," Karim said. He walked with her to the car and unloaded baseballs, bats, gloves, basketballs, footballs, and other sports equipment. "Where did you get all this stuff?"

"I've kept these things for years," she explained. "I didn't want to part with them because they belonged to my late son. He was a wonderful athlete. Do you know that he played in the very first basketball game at Bellwood High? That's when the school had less than a hundred kids and very little money. They didn't even have a gym, so they used to practice here. He spent so much time here shooting baskets until late at night."

Her eyes had a faraway look as she continued. "The team didn't do too well the first two years. But in his senior year, the team nearly went undefeated. My son was the star. They went all the way to the state finals and they were on TV. There was a huge crowd at the university arena, and everybody was pulling for Bellwood. Yes, it was quite a game."

"Did Bellwood win?"

She lowered her eyes and replied softly, "No, they lost by a single point. It was a tearjerker." She stared off in space for a moment before clearing her throat. "Well, I must be going. Please put his equipment to good use."

"We will, ma'am. Thank you."

Back inside the warehouse, Karim was storing the equipment when he dropped a heavy duffle bag. Among the items that spilled out was a folder stuffed with old newspaper clippings about Bellwood High's basketball team. One undated article came from the front page of the *Bellwood Weekly*. It said:

LOCAL HOOPSTERS' DREAM SEASON SHATTERED
Lose in State Finals, 45–44

Bellwood High came within two free throws of capping an amazing season last Saturday before falling to Asheboro 45–44 in the state finals.

Bellwood's Orlando Huckaby, who had scored 23 points to lead the Rams, stepped to the foul line for two free throws with only one second remaining and his team trailing by a single point. One free throw would tie the game. Two would bring Bellwood the state championship.

But the crushing pressure apparently was too great. He missed them both.

Is this the same Orlando Huckaby that I met? Karim wondered. *It has to be. That explains why he said those things to me. I've got to ask him about this the next time I see him.*

Karim's eyes fell on the accompanying photo. It showed a basketball player sitting by his locker, his head in his hands. His face was hidden. The caption read: "Bellwood star Orlando Huckaby weeps tears of anguish moments after the Rams' gut-wrenching 45–44 loss."

45–44? thought Karim. *That's what the scoreboard said both times when it lit up on its own! This is getting really strange.*

A sickening sensation hit Karim in the stomach. *Hold on. The old lady said this stuff belonged to her late son. That means he's dead. But Orlando can't be dead. I've seen him. So whose stuff is this?*

As he picked up the duffle bag, he noticed a tag on the strap. Scrawled in pen was the name SGT. ORLANDO HUCKABY.

Frightened and bewildered, Karim quickly stuffed the duffle bag onto a shelf. He dashed out of the youth center and ran straight to George's house.

"George, do you know Orlando Huckaby?" Karim asked anxiously.

"I knew him. We were on the same basketball team at Bellwood High. He was the star. I was a reserve."

"Do you know where I can find him?"

"Probably at Bellwood Cemetery. He was killed in the Vietnam War around 1970. He earned a Medal of Honor for valor after rescuing his entire platoon from an ambush, but it cost him his life. He was quite a hero. The town even named a park after him."

"We can't be talking about the same person, George.

Orlando is about twenty years old, tall, muscular, a shaved head with a big scar across his forehead."

George crooked his finger. "Follow me." He took Karim into the den and pointed to a photograph of ten high school basketball players sitting on the bleachers. "That's the team picture from the 1967–68 season, when we went to the state finals. There's Orlando in the center."

Karim stared awestruck at the photo. "It . . . it c-c-can't be," he stammered. "It's impossible. He's the one I've seen at the youth center! I've talked to him twice."

"You saw Orlando?"

Karim nodded. "Honest, I did."

"Karim, I'm going to tell you something that might frighten you. You saw Orlando's ghost."

Karim's knees felt like they were about to buckle. "His ghost?"

"You're not the first to have seen Orlando's ghost at the warehouse. He's been spotted at least four times over the past twenty-five years. I think his soul finds comfort there because of all the time he spent practicing in that gym."

"So why did he show up for me?"

"I don't know, Karim. His ghost obviously felt a certain kinship with you, a connection."

"Well, we both embarrassed ourselves in games."

"Oh, so you know what happened at the state finals."

"Yeah, 45–44," said Karim. Then his eyes grew wide. "The state university donated the scoreboard, right? Could this have been the one that was used when Bellwood played in the state finals?"

"It's about thirty years old, so, yes, it could have been."

"It's all starting to make sense to me, George. When

Orlando's ghost shows up at the center, the board flashes the score of the worst moment in his life as a player. And now he's trying to help me cope with my worst moment."

At the Falcons' next home game against the Stockton Pirates, Hacker and two other starters fouled out, allowing Karim to play during crunch time of another tight battle. In the final five minutes, he sparked a rally by grabbing five rebounds and scoring four points. Then, with time running out and his team down by one point, Karim stole the ball but was fouled as he tried to make a layup.

Karim went to the free throw line with only one second left in the game. He nervously bounced the ball several times and told himself, *If I make both shots, we win and I become a hero. If I miss them both, I'm the goat—again. One out of two and we go into overtime. Let me make at least one, please!*

He wiped his sweaty palms on the sides of his shorts and bounced the ball a few more times. Then Karim launched the ball, showing excellent form. The shot had the right height and the proper arc. But it didn't have enough distance and glanced off the front of the rim.

His teammates groaned just loud enough for Karim to hear. Then they clapped encouragingly. "Come on, Karim." "Sink this one." "Make it for the tie."

But the Pirates hissed, "You're gonna blow it!" "Don't choke!" "Miss it!"

The pressure building by the second, Karim wasted little time on his next shot. He tossed up the ball harder. It banged off the back of the rim, bounced up, hit the rim again—and fell off the side.

The Falcons had lost another one. And once again, Karim took the blame. *I'm never playing this game again,* Karim said angrily to himself. *Never, ever. I hate it. I'm such a loser. I'm such a bad—*

Suddenly a cold draft brushed across Karim's shoulders. Someone was standing just behind him, Karim was sure of it. But when he whirled around, he saw nothing but the scoreboard. It read: VISITORS 45, HOME 44.

"Remember what I told you," a ghostly voice whispered in his ear.

Orlando? Karim thought. Then he recalled the pep talk the ghost had given him after Karim had humiliated himself during the game against the Jaguars: *What happened today is nothing more than proof that you are human and not perfect. Don't let it get you down. Keep plugging away. If you don't find success here, you'll find it somewhere else. Your worth as a person is not judged on how well you perform on the basketball court.*

Karim's anguish started to ease and a grin crossed his face. "Thanks, Orlando," he said out loud. Then, holding his head high, Karim walked back to the bench, thinking, *Maybe I'll go out for the school baseball team next spring.*

THE MAN IN BLUE

Come on, Colby, keep moving! Faster! Faster!

The strained muscles in Colby Vance's legs burned in protest as the sophomore cross-country runner headed up the ever-steepening path. He hated this part of the course. He had already run over three miles (4.8 km), and now he faced the most difficult challenge of this practice race—Screech Hill.

The runners had given the hill that name because so many of them felt like screaming in pain during the torturous climb. The hill marked the start of the final leg of the course. Here was where the mind had to take over the body.

The lean, curly-haired fifteen-year-old whipped his bandanna off his neck and wiped his sweaty face. *Block out the pain! Keep going! Keep pumping! Breathe. Breathe. Think of something else, anything . . . think of . . . that strange man over there.*

A man in his fifties leaned against a poplar tree about ten yards (9.1 m) off the flagged cross-country course. He was dressed completely in pale blue, from his pale blue long-sleeved collarless shirt to his matching pale blue pants and shoes. His combed-back, snow-white hair curled near the nape of his neck and brushed over the tops of his ears. Slender sideburns linked his hair to a close-cropped white beard that framed his square jaw.

Colby and his fellow runners seldom saw anyone during their practice runs through the rolling, wooded hills in the park behind their school. Cross-country running was not exactly a top spectator sport. The only audience was usually parents and friends at competitive meets—and they most often stood at the start and finish line rather than on the course.

The man in blue didn't look like the typical cross-country spectator. He certainly wasn't dressed for a walk in the woods. Colby had never seen him before, and the runner wondered why the man's eyes—so light they seemed colorless—were locked directly onto him. The man's fair-skinned face—free of wrinkles despite his age—gave no hint of emotion, although Colby had a feeling the stranger was a kind, gentle person.

Colby kept his gaze on the man and failed to notice a large root sticking out onto the path. He stumbled badly but managed to keep his balance and regain his stride.

When Colby looked toward the poplar tree again, the man had disappeared. Colby kept running while his eyes searched among the trees for the strange man in blue.

"Colby, you're running like an old lady! Pick up the pace!" shouted Coach Barry Stern, zipping down the trail in his golf cart. That was how he kept tabs on his runners.

"Easy for you to say," Colby muttered under his breath. Colby didn't think anything more about the man in blue. But he would later.

❦　　❦　　❦

Colby loved to run. He had the perfect build and mentality for cross-country. Somewhat of a loner, he wasn't fond of team sports. He lacked the skills for basketball and baseball and was too skinny for football. So cross-country running suited him fine. It wasn't as popular as other sports, but that was all right with him. Colby competed for himself, always trying to better his time.

Colby lived with his parents, Doreen and Benton, and his brother, Chandler, far out in the country. Their small, wood-frame house sat on stilts above palmetto plants and thick brush that was home to wild animals such as raccoons, opossums, wildcats, and foxes. The woods behind their house provided shelter for deer and even bears. The woods also teemed with deadly snakes— rattlers, water moccasins, and copperheads. Their mother always warned Colby and Chandler of the dangers of snakes. Colby had seen plenty of them in the woods and tried his best to avoid them.

When he trained near home, he sometimes ran on the gravel road that led to the nearby highway toward town. But he found that route boring, and he hated breathing the choking dust kicked up by passing pickup trucks and cars. Instead, he liked to run in the woods on an overgrown road that once serviced an orange grove. It was a five-mile (8-km) run on the grove road from his house to an old irrigation ditch and back.

One Saturday morning, Colby donned his running shoes for a jaunt in the woods. The last wispy traces of fog on this sunny, cool day moved lazily through the trees. *I feel real good today. Let's see if I can shave fifteen seconds off my best time,* he thought.

"Mom, I'm going for a run in the grove," Colby shouted.

"You'd best be careful," replied Doreen. "Those snakes will be out sunning themselves this time of day."

"Your sssssson will be ssssssssafe," Colby joked, deliberately emphasizing the sound of a snake.

He opened the back door and bounded down the steps to the yard below, where he began doing his stretching exercises. Moments later, he set his watch and headed onto the grove road. Two scrub jays squawked at him from a nearby tree.

The long torpedo grass on the grove road had grown to nearly six inches (15 cm), and the blades tickled the tops of his ankles with every step. *This is one of those days when my engine is just purring,* Colby thought as he ran. *I feel strong. I feel fast . . . There's the ditch up ahead.*

As he jumped across the shallow trench, Colby's right foot landed on a rubbery object. His ankle twisted, and he fell.

An instant later, a burning pain shot through his foot. He looked down and gasped in horror. He was staring at the biggest, ugliest, meanest snake he had ever seen in his life—a six-foot-long (1.8-m) diamondback rattler. It was so huge that its mouth covered Colby's entire right shoe up to the laces. The snake's razor-sharp fangs had pierced deep through Colby's shoe and thick cotton sock, straight into his skin.

Normally, a rattler will try to strike at its victim two or three times, but this snake couldn't get its mouth off Colby's foot because its fangs were snagged on his sock. Screaming in terror and pain, Colby hopped around on his left foot, trying desperately to shake the deadly reptile off his right foot. But the snake locked its jaws and relentlessly pumped more of its lethal venom into his body.

As the pain grew more intense, Colby shrieked, "Get off! Get off! Get off!" He reached for a dead branch and used it to beat the snake until it finally released its deadly grip. The rattler then slithered off into the brush.

An agonizing burning sensation crawled through Colby's right foot and into his leg. *I'm going to die!* he told himself. *There's no way I can survive a bite from a rattler that big. Oh, it hurts!* Then he remembered what his mother had always taught him: If you get bit by a snake, stay calm and don't take off running.

I can't panic now, Colby thought. *I've got to make it back to the house. If I don't, nobody will find me in time. I'll die right here. It's only a short distance. I can do it.*

He tried to walk but managed to stagger only a few steps. The throbbing fireball of pain was spreading through his body. *Stay calm. But how can I? It hurts so much. How can I walk that far?* He tried to block out the stories he had heard about people who suffered horrifying deaths from the bites of killer snakes.

Breathing became a chore. Colby felt as though an invisible vise was squeezing all the air out of his aching lungs. His heart was pumping so wildly from fright and pain that he feared it would explode.

I've got to get home before I die. He took another couple of shaky, painful steps, dragging his right foot. But the effort left him so weak, he could barely stand. Colby's head was spinning. His eyes fluttered and his body began to shake from shock. *I'm not going to make it. It's too far and I hurt too much.* In that instant, Colby was about to give up. He wanted to surrender to the pain, let himself slip into unconsciousness, and wait for death.

Unexpectedly, he heard a man's voice behind him say, "Don't give up."

Colby's vision and hearing were rapidly failing. "Is somebody here? Can you help me?" He was too weak to see where the voice was coming from.

"Let me help you."

Colby couldn't stand any longer. His right leg buckled, pitching his body to the side. Colby winced, anticipating the impact of slamming onto the ground. But he never hit the path. Instead, he felt himself land in a pair of strong, steady, comforting arms.

Colby looked up. Through his blurred vision, he saw the face of a white-haired, white-bearded man whose eyes were nearly colorless.

"You're the man in blue," mumbled Colby, "the man I saw in the park."

The man, who was wearing the same pale blue long-sleeved collarless shirt, smiled and replied, "Yes, I am."

"I've been bit by a rattler. I'm dying."

"You must relax your body. You must stay strong in your mind, just like you do when you're running."

"Who are you?"

"Someone who will help you back to your house."

The man carried Colby in his arms as if he were holding a baby. Colby had the bizarre feeling that the man in blue was floating. Colby never felt him take any steps. Everything seemed so smooth as they moved through the woods.

What's happening to me? he asked himself. *I must be*

imagining this. Or maybe I'm dead. But the stinging poison that kept coursing through his body told him otherwise.

I must be hallucinating, Colby thought as he and the man in blue floated along. *Either that or he's a ghost.* Colby stammered, "Am . . . I . . . dead . . . yet?"

"No, Colby, you're not dead," the man replied. "You're in bad shape, however. You must use your mind and heart to stay alive. If you do your part and I do mine, you'll make it."

The man's voice sounded like nothing Colby had ever heard before. It was velvety yet deep, clear yet distant.

Colby relaxed. The pain eased as shock took over his body. Somehow he knew that, no matter how bleak his situation looked at the moment, he was going to survive.

In less time than he could imagine, Colby reached the top of the stairs by the back door of his house. The man in blue gently set him down and said, "You're going to live."

Still stunned by all that had happened to him over the last few minutes, Colby, on all fours, opened the door. Just then, the pain returned with a vengeance. He crawled into the living room and cried out to his brother, "Chandler, a rattler bit me. This kind man brought me home." Then Colby passed out on the floor.

"Is this a joke?" asked Chandler. He got up from his chair and looked outside. No one was there. Then he bent down to check his brother and knew immediately this was no laughing matter.

"Mama! Hurry! It's Colby! He got bit by a snake!"

Doreen rushed into the room, ripped the shoe off her son's foot, and smelled the distinctive, musky odor of rattlesnake venom. Colby's entire foot had already turned deep purple and was swelling. "Oh, no!" Doreen cried. "The fang marks are so far apart!"

"What's that mean, Mama?" asked Chandler.

"It means a huge rattler bit Colby."

Doreen, who had some nursing experience, felt sick to her stomach when she looked closely at the wound. The fangs had pierced a vein in Colby's ankle, causing the venom to spread quickly. She could barely detect Colby's pulse. "His body is shutting down," she told Chandler. "We've got to get him to the hospital right now!"

The family had no phone and lived far from any neighbors who had one. The nearest hospital was at least twenty miles (32.3 km) away.

Chandler ran outside and told his father, Benton, what had happened. Benton raced up the steps, scooped up his dying son, and carried him down to the family's only vehicle, a beat-up pickup truck. Benton drove as Colby lay across the laps of his mother, brother, and father in the front seat.

Doreen held her son's head close to hers to monitor his shallow breathing, which was growing weaker by the minute.

"He's hardly breathing at all!" she shouted frantically. "We've got to get to the hospital fast!" Suddenly, Colby's body began to shake uncontrollably. "Now he's gone into convulsions!" she cried. "Step on it!"

Doreen tried hard not to panic or think of how her son was only minutes away from death. She felt so afraid, so helpless that there was nothing more she could do for him. "Colby, you can't die!" she demanded. "You just can't!"

"Oh, no!" shouted Benton. "The engine is overheating!"

"You can't stop!" Doreen declared. "We've got to get him to the hospital!"

"Okay, I'll keep it floored."

But within a minute, the engine began to knock badly, then sputtered and died. When the truck rolled to a stop, Benton jumped out and tried to hail a passing motorist, but the car drove past him without stopping.

"We've got to do something fast!" Doreen pleaded.

In desperation, Benton lifted Colby out of the truck, held him in his arms, and stood in the middle of the highway. Within moments, a shiny new light blue Mercedes sedan slowed to a stop.

"My son is dying from a snake bite," Benton shouted. "My truck broke down. You've got to take us to the hospital!"

"By all means," said the driver. "Get in!"

The family piled into the backseat and, with Colby stretched across their laps, headed to the hospital.

Colby briefly regained consciousness and groaned. "I'm cold," he whispered, his body still quivering. "So cold."

"Please, oh, please, hurry!" Doreen begged the driver. "Every second counts. I'm so afraid that by the time we reach the emergency room, it'll be too late for Colby."

"We'll make it in time," said the driver. "Trust me."

Before he passed out again, Colby tried to say something to his mother, but Doreen couldn't understand him. She thought she heard him utter the words "man" and "blue."

Minutes later, the car roared up to the hospital. By the time Colby was wheeled into the emergency room, his condition had worsened. His arms, legs, and feet had ballooned to twice their normal size. His face was so badly swollen that blood seeped out of his nose and the sides of his eyes. His heart rate was too high and his blood pressure and respiratory rate were too low.

Three doctors and two nurses feverishly joined in a valiant effort to save Colby's life. They put him on a ventilator—a machine to help him breathe—and hooked him up to monitoring devices and IV tubes. While trying to stabilize him, they injected him with anti-venom serum, a gold-colored liquid designed to counteract the snake's deadly poison.

After working on Colby for over an hour, Dr. Ray Brook, a critical-care specialist, left the emergency room to talk to Doreen and Benton. "Colby is still critical and we've done all that we can do right now," said the doctor. "He should have died before he even got here. I treat snake bites on a regular basis, and this is the worst one I've ever seen."

Dr. Brook told the family the venom had affected all of Colby's bodily systems—heart, lung, brain, kidney. "But we've given him the anti-venom serum and kept him alive. Now it's just a matter of waiting to see what happens to his organs, especially his kidneys. Is he a fighter? Does he have the will to live?"

"He's tough," replied Benton. "My son has great willpower. He runs at least five miles [8 km] a day, rain or shine."

"Good," said the doctor, "because he's in a race for his life."

Colby was moved to a room in intensive care, where he remained on a ventilator. Later that day, he finally regained consciousness. Over the next twenty-four hours, he steadily improved until he could breathe on his own.

When Colby was unhooked from the ventilator, his relieved mother asked him, "How do you feel, sweetheart?"

"I hurt all over, but I'll be okay," he replied. Then he described in detail his near-fatal encounter with the rattlesnake.

"I don't know how you managed to make it back to the house," she said.

"I made it because of that nice man."

"What nice man?"

"The man who found me in the woods and carried me back to the house. Didn't you see him?"

"No, Colby. There wasn't anyone out there."

"Why would he leave like that?"

"Are you sure you didn't imagine him?"

"No, because I had seen him once before, at the park during practice last week. After I got bit by the snake, the man just appeared out of nowhere. He was in his fifties, dressed all in blue, and had white hair and . . ."

". . . and a white beard and very pale eyes?"

"Yes, that's the man. Do you know him?"

"When our truck conked out on the way to the hospital, we flagged a man down who fits that description. But he never said a word about rescuing you. If he was the same man who helped you, why wouldn't he have stayed with you at the house? Why wouldn't he have told us in the car that he found you right after you got bit?"

"Did you get his name, Mama? Do you know who he is?"

"No, we rushed you straight into the emergency room.

When we finally went into the waiting room, he was gone. Nobody else even remembers seeing him."

"He's strange. He's different." Then Colby looked his mother squarely in the eye and asked, "Mama, will you believe me if I tell you something very weird?"

"Of course, Colby."

"After I got bit by the snake, the man picked me up in his arms, and, Mama, I swear he was floating, not walking! I think he was a ghost!"

Doreen's face clearly showed her bewilderment. She stroked Colby's forehead. "Maybe you should get some rest, okay? We'll talk about this later."

"But I'm telling the truth."

"You've gone through an awful lot, and with all the medication and everything—"

"Mama, didn't that man seem strange to you, like maybe he wasn't human?"

"Well, he had a certain presence about him that I can't describe. He had a very calming effect on us and kept reassuring us that everything would be okay. The way he said it, I truly believed him."

Colby threw back the covers and looked at his swollen right foot. The sight made him cringe.

"Do you think I'll ever be able to run again?"

"Don't worry," his mother replied. "The doctors will fix up your foot. You'll be running before you know it—but not in the grove. Now get some rest."

Colby fell into a deep sleep. But in the middle of the night, he woke up for no apparent reason. As his eyes adjusted to the night light, he tried to figure out where he was.

"You're going to be fine," said a familiar voice.

Startled, Colby turned to his right and squinted. The man in blue stepped out from a dark corner of the room.

"You're the man who saved my life," said Colby.

The man bowed in acknowledgment.

"How can I ever repay you for what you did?"

"Pay me back by running cross-country again."

"With this foot? Fat chance."

"That's my price. And I expect to be paid in full."

"The doctors said I suffered severe nerve damage in my foot and . . ." As Colby spoke, the door creaked open and a nurse stepped inside the room.

"Are you awake or are you talking in your sleep?" she whispered to Colby.

He turned his head to the left and told her, "I'm awake. I'm talking to my friend here."

"A visitor? At two A.M.?" The nurse turned on the light and raised her eyebrows. There was no one else in the room.

"Hey, where did he go?" asked Colby, trying to sit up. "I was talking to him a second ago. You had to have seen him—a man in his fifties, with white hair and a beard."

The nurse just shook her head. She checked Colby's vital signs and left the room.

Could I have been dreaming? wondered Colby. *I sure wish I could see him again. I sure wish I knew who he is . . . and what he is.*

After two operations and months of therapy, Colby made a complete recovery. "The odds were very much against you," Dr. Brook told him. "Your survival was incredible. Most people wouldn't have lived through what you experienced." He put his hand on Colby's shoulder. "Now I'm giving you permission to run cross-country."

Following months of training, Colby returned to the team in his junior year. He considered it a major triumph when he ran in his first competitive race—a four-miler (6.4 km)—since the snake bite. In the first mile (1.6 km), he stayed in the middle of the pack. He moved up near the leaders after the third mile (4.8 km). With a quarter mile (.4 km) to go, Colby poured it on. His finishing kick on the final stretch had him breathing down the leader's neck.

Colby's leg muscles screamed in protest as he burst into the lead with 100 yards (91 km) to go. His lungs aching, his arms pumping, Colby lunged across the finish line four seconds ahead of his nearest competitor.

Victory never felt so good. He raised his arms in triumph while a swarm of family and friends hugged and kissed him. Then, from the fringe of the well-wishers, he heard a distinctive voice say, "Consider yourself having paid me in full."

Colby gazed over the heads of his family and friends and broke out in a broad grin. The man in blue gave a wink and a wave. "Hi!" yelled Colby. "Let me shake your hand."

Doreen had no idea the man was there. She grabbed her sweaty son and spun him around, saying, "Smile for the photographer." Colby flashed a quick grin and then broke free a second after the click of the shutter, hoping to find the man in blue.

But it was no use. The man in blue had vanished once again. Then, to the surprise of everyone, Colby shouted, "I guess I did pay you back . . . whoever you are!"

TEAMMATE FROM BEYOND

That's it? That's as fast as you can throw?" heckled Ellie Maucker after catching a pitch from Cami Blake.

"Of course not," Cami shouted back from the mound. "That was just a warm-up toss. Get ready for some real heat."

Ellie squatted behind the plate and pounded her catcher's glove. "Okay, fire it right in here."

The willowy right-handed pitcher made a short rocking motion on the mound and then whipped the ball underhanded. It blazed across the plate and smacked into Ellie's mitt with a loud pop.

Ellie stood up and flipped the ball back to Cami. "Not bad, but I've seen better."

"Where? In the major leagues?"

"No, Little League."

Both girls burst out laughing. They were meeting for the first time on the softball field at Simms High School, where they were both juniors. Softball coach Sally Thomas wanted the two girls to spend time together so they would trust and understand each other on the field and think as one. They needed to be in sync because Ellie would be calling the pitches for Cami.

"What number do you want on your jersey?" Ellie asked.

"Two."

"Sorry. That's my favorite number. On official scorecards, the number two means catcher."

"And number one means pitcher," Cami reminded her. "So the pitcher is obviously the most important person on the team. Yeah, I think I'll ask for number one."

Appearance-wise, the two girls were a picture of stark contrasts. Cami, tall and slender, moved with grace and style. Her almond-shaped green eyes and high cheekbones gave her an exotic flair that seemed more suited for the fashion runway than the baseball diamond. On the field, she tied her cover-girl blonde hair into a ponytail that flowed from the back of her baseball cap. Ellie had a catcher's body—short and stocky. Her curly, thick, black hair tumbled down onto a chubby face that featured dimples and big brown eyes. Surprisingly agile for a girl of her build, Ellie could really clobber the ball.

"You know, Cami, you're good," said Ellie after their first practice together. "But you could be a lot better."

"Well, of course there's always room for improvement," Cami replied, slightly miffed.

"What you need is a good drop ball. You could really be a top pitcher if you add a drop ball to your fastball and change-up."

"But I don't know how to throw one."

"Stick with me, kid. I'll teach you."

Within a week, Ellie had taught Cami how to put spin

on the ball so it would drop as it reached the plate. The catcher also gave her a few pointers on how to improve her change-up—a pitch that is delivered like a fastball but is much slower.

About two weeks after they first met, Cami showed up unexpectedly at Ellie's house and held up a makeup bag. "You showed me how to improve my change-up technique," Cami said. "Now I'm going to show you how to improve your makeup technique."

"What are you talking about?"

"Ellie, you have an adorable face. But you use makeup as if you were hiding behind a catcher's mask."

"Let's face it, Cami. I'm not exactly Miss Glamour."

"Oh, you will be by the time we're done. Besides, you have to look good for Gary Buckner."

"Gary? He's going with Cindy Stewart."

"Not anymore. And the word around school is that he has his fetching blue eyes on a certain very cute catcher."

"No way!"

"Let's get you in front of a mirror and bring out your best features."

"My best feature is I can catch and hit long balls."

"Well, when we get finished, you'll be catching more than pitches. Just do me a favor. Lose the patchouli oil."

"But that's my favorite perfume. My mom wore it in the sixties."

"Well, it's the nineties now."

"There are some things I won't do, and one of them is give up my patchouli oil. That's my scent. That's me."

"Will you at least consider changing to a lighter, more delicate perfume like my Charlemagne?"

"I'll tell you what. I'll switch to Charlemagne the day you twirl a no-no."

"A no-hitter? It's a deal."

From then on, the two girls developed a great friendship and often double-dated—Cami with a different boy almost every month, and Ellie with her new steady Gary.

Meanwhile, on the field, the dynamic duo seemed unbeatable. Mixing her fastball and change-up with her new drop ball, Cami won nine games and lost only two. Meanwhile, Ellie led the team in homers with twelve as Simms captured the league championship.

"The next stop is the state tournament," Ellie told Cami. "To win the state title has always been my dream. I'm going to be on the winning team—or die trying!"

Behind Cami's strong pitching, the Eagles won the first game of the state tournament, 5–2. In the next contest, Ellie clubbed two doubles and drove in three runs in a 6–4 victory.

While getting ready in the locker room for the semifinal game against the tough Henderson High Blazers, Cami noticed Ellie wincing as she tied her shoes.

"What's wrong, Ellie?"

"Oh, nothing. My back is acting up a little. Probably from carrying this team the whole season," she joked. Ellie tugged on her unicorn earrings and grinned. "We're getting so close to that title. We've got to win today."

"Don't worry. We will. I'm on the mound, remember?"

Ellie dabbed on a little patchouli oil like she did before every game. And, in what was a pregame ritual, Cami always gagged. "You're gassing us out of the room, Ellie."

"This is my good-luck potion. That's what will help

us win—patchouli and my lucky unicorn earrings."

The seven-inning game turned into a nail-biter. Both hurlers were locked in a scoreless duel, each having scattered four hits through six innings. The Eagles threatened to win it in the top of the seventh, putting runners on first and second with one out and Ellie at the plate. It looked promising—until she hit a grounder. On her swing, Ellie cried out in pain, causing her to get a late start out of the batter's box. Meanwhile, the ball bounced to the shortstop, who fielded it, stepped on second, and fired to first to nip Ellie by a half step in an inning-ending double play.

Cami and Coach Thomas hurried over to Ellie, who was walking slowly toward the dugout with her hands on her lower back. "I must have pulled a muscle," she told them. "I'll be all right."

"Maybe I should take you out of the game," Coach Thomas said.

"No, you can't," Ellie pleaded. "This means so much. A win today puts us in the finals. I've worked too hard to get here. I'm fine, Coach. Honest." Then, speaking out of the side of her mouth, she lowered her voice and said, "Just between us, Coach, Cami wouldn't know what to do without me. I have to tell her everything."

Overhearing Ellie's joke, Cami cracked up and said, "If you take Ellie out, she'll finally know the truth—that I don't need her to win. And that will devastate her."

As the teammates giggled, Coach Thomas shook her head and said, "Oh, all right, Ellie. Get in there."

The bottom of the seventh started badly for Simms High. A short pop fly fell between three diving Eagles. Then the next Blazers batter hit a "seeing-eye" grounder that skipped past the shortstop and the third baseman. The winning run now stood on second base. A solid base hit could end the Eagles' dream of playing in the state finals.

Cami circled the mound to collect her thoughts and stay calm. One bad pitch and it would be all over. She gulped. Her mouth tasted like infield dirt.

Ellie called time and walked to the mound. "You do intend to get the next three batters out, don't you?" she asked Cami.

"Only if you start calling the right pitches."

"Actually, I thought—for the sake of the crowd—we should add a little excitement. Let's walk the next batter to load the bases . . ."

". . . and get a three-ball, no-strike count on the following batter before I strike out the side."

"Sounds like a good plan to me." Ellie turned and headed back to her position behind the plate. Regaining control of her nerves, Cami took a couple of deep breaths. She couldn't help but notice that Ellie was walking as if she were in a lot of pain.

Cami didn't quite follow the game plan, although she did strike out the next batter and coax the following hitter to pop up. Now there were two out and two on.

"One more, Cami! One more!" hollered Ellie.

The next batter stroked a clean single to left. The runner on second—the winning run—dashed around third and streaked for home. Eagles left fielder Patty Johnson cleanly scooped up the ball and pegged a perfect throw home.

Ellie caught the ball, blocked the plate, and braced for the collision at home. When the runner crashed into Ellie, the impact sent the catcher reeling. Ellie landed hard on her back, triggering a sharp pain along her spine. Looming over the play, the umpire was about to call the runner out when he noticed the ball had trickled out of Ellie's mitt. He spread out his hands and shouted, "Safe!" The Blazers had won, 1–0.

The shock of losing the heartbreaker hit Cami in the pit of her stomach. She felt empty and helpless. If only she could push the rewind button on a magical VCR so that she could have another chance at getting the batter out.

I hate those Blazers, she thought, tears streaming down her face. *Look at them, jumping up and down, hugging each other. That should have been us. They're so happy and . . . Is that Ellie still on the ground?*

Cami, followed by her teammates and Coach Thomas, rushed over to their catcher, who was writhing in pain near home plate.

"I can't move!" Ellie cried. "My back hurts!"

A doctor jumped out of the stands and tended to Ellie. She was placed on a stretcher and taken to the hospital for a battery of tests.

When Cami was finally allowed to visit, she was startled at Ellie's appearance. Ellie was drawn and pale. She lay in her bed with her arms connected to IVs.

"I let everyone down, Cami, including myself," Ellie said weakly. "I should've held on to the ball."

"You're not to blame. I am. My drop ball didn't drop."

"Yeah, I guess it was all your fault," Ellie deadpanned. "Your pitch was too fat."

"Oh, yeah?" a smirking Cami retorted. "You let that prissy little runner knock you into the tenth row. What kind of catcher are you?"

Cami bent over and buried her head on Ellie's chest and they both sobbed. After their tears had ended, Ellie asked, "Hey, why were you bawling?"

"Because I hate seeing you like this."

"I hate seeing me like this too."

"Is that why you were crying, Ellie?"

"No, I'm just upset because I lost one of my unicorn earrings in the collision."

"C'mon, Ellie. What's the real reason?"

"Because we lost our chance to go to the championship. It's the only thing I ever wanted. Cami, we had it in the palm of my hand."

"We'll be back next year."

"Sure you will."

"*We* will," Cami corrected her. Ellie nodded and forced a smile.

"When are you getting out of here?" asked Cami. Ellie turned her head away. "Ellie, what's wrong?"

"Picture this: two outs in the last inning, trailing by four runs, nobody on base, and I'm at the plate facing an 0-and-2 count. It doesn't look good."

"Ellie, what are you saying?"

"The truth is, Cami, the doctors found a nasty tumor on my spine. It's cancer and it's bad, real bad. The doctors say it's terminal and there's nothing they can do about it."

Seeing Cami's shocked expression, Ellie managed to joke, "Hey, look at the bright side. I won't have to catch your dumb drop balls anymore."

"Don't talk like that, Ellie. We need you. I need you. You're my best friend."

"Don't worry, Cami. I'll be haunting you on the field.

You know you can't win without me. I'll be your batterymate from the other side, that's all. We have a championship to win next year."

The disease spread mercilessly through Ellie's body. Two months after the semifinal game, the Eagles' catcher died.

For her senior softball season at Simms High, Cami had to get used to a new catcher. Stacy Moore didn't have Ellie's wry sense of humor or her power at the plate. But Stacy was a clutch hitter, had a rifle arm, and knew how to call a good game.

The Eagles dedicated the season to Ellie's memory. They had a black patch with the number 2 sewn on the left sleeve of their jerseys in her honor.

As luck would have it, their first game of the year was on the field where they had suffered the gut-wrenching semifinal defeat. During batting practice, Cami walked toward home plate—the scene of that terrible collision.

Cami closed her eyes and tried to talk to Ellie's spirit: "I don't know where you are or what you're doing, but you better not be teaching anyone else the drop ball, Ellie. I really miss you. You're my teammate, and I need you with me. How about if you stick by me this whole season—all the way to the state finals, okay? We can't win the championship without you. Give me some of your goofy guidance when I get in trouble. And, oh, one other thing. Give me a sign that you're listening."

Cami opened her eyes and started to walk toward the dugout. As she passed a groundskeeper raking the area near home plate, she noticed a tiny object glittering in the dirt. She picked it up and then began to laugh and cry at the same time. It was the unicorn earring that Ellie had lost after the collision.

"Oh, Ellie, thank you! Now I know you'll be with me the whole season. Let's go win ourselves a championship!"

Cami tucked her glove under her arm, took off her right earring and replaced it with the unicorn earring. She would wear it during every game.

Throughout the season, Cami felt Ellie's presence on the field, although she never saw or heard Ellie's ghost. Whenever she found herself in a pitching jam, Cami would carry on a brief conversation with her former batterymate. It helped the hurler stay cool and collected on the mound. And it helped her win.

Cami spearheaded a fantastic year for the Simms High Eagles. They breezed through the conference undefeated and sported a regular-season record of 23–2. Named the league's most valuable player for her spotless 15–0 record, Cami pitched five shutouts and tossed three two-hitters.

The Eagles returned to the state playoffs, determined to capture the title. After winning the first two games in the tourney, they once again faced the Henderson High Blazers, last year's state champs and the team that had knocked the Eagles out of the playoffs.

Before the Blazers' leadoff batter stepped up to the plate, Cami stood on the mound and tugged at the unicorn earring dangling from her right ear. "Just like old times, huh, Ellie? But this time the outcome will be different. We'll beat the Blazers and get our revenge. We'll win for ourselves— and for you."

The game turned into a classic pitcher's duel and was scoreless after five and a half innings. In the bottom of the sixth, Cami kneeled in the ondeck circle and had another chat with Ellie's spirit: "I don't know if you have any clout from the beyond, but if you do, it sure would be nice if you could find a way to help us win."

Moments later, with one out and no one on base, Cami hit a blooper behind third base. The left fielder charged in and the third baseman ran out—and they smacked into each other. The ball dropped safely, and Cami ended up on second. "Not bad, Ellie," whispered Cami. "That's a good start."

Stacy Moore then knocked in Cami by ripping a shot that struck the bag at first and bounced over the first baseman and down the right field line for another lucky double.

"Now you're cooking, Ellie," said Cami as she crossed the plate. One batter later, Patty Johnson blasted a home run over the center field wall, giving the Eagles a 3–0 cushion.

In the top of the final inning, Cami tingled with the anticipation of beating the Blazers. "We're only three outs away, Ellie. Can you believe it?" She fooled the first batter into popping out. But the excitement of being so close to victory caused Cami to lose her concentration. She walked the next batter. Then, after shaking off Stacy's signal for a fastball, Cami threw a change-up that didn't fool the hitter. The Blazer teed off on the pitch and launched it over the left field wall for a two-run homer. Now it was 3–2.

Coach Thomas called time and hustled out to the mound. "Are you getting tired, Cami?"

"No, I just lost my concentration. I got too excited. But I feel strong. I'll get them out."

"Then go do it!" The coach patted her on the rear and headed back to the dugout.

Maybe I'll go with the drop ball on this batter. No, she's a low ball . . . Suddenly, Cami became aware that everything was silent. She saw her teammates mouthing their infield chatter. She saw people in the stands clapping and stomping. She saw the Blazers' bench jockeys spewing their trash talk. But Cami couldn't hear anyone or anything.

Before she had a chance to panic, Cami heard a voice in her head—a voice that was dear to her heart: "Don't throw any more change-ups like that gopher ball you served up. The way you telegraphed that pitch, you might as well carry a neon sign telling the batter what's coming. Go with your best stuff—the fastball. Get these bozos out!"

Ellie's voice was as clear as if she were standing there on the mound, her hands on her hips, one hand holding her mitt and the other her mask. "Come on, Cami, two outs to go. You know how much I love the number two. Deuces wild."

Suddenly, Cami heard the infield chatter, the bench jockeying, and the crowd again.

"Young lady, do you plan to pitch any time within the next hour?" the home-plate umpire asked sarcastically.

"Oh, yes, of course."

Cami felt a rush of confidence. *Ellie's spirit is with me here on the mound! How can I possibly lose?* She settled down and, throwing nothing but fastballs, struck out the next two batters to win the game. The Eagles had made it to the state championship game!

The Simms players rushed out to the mound and hugged Cami. "We did it! We did it! We beat the state champs! This is our year to win it all!"

As the players danced their way toward the dugout, Cami stayed on the mound. "Thanks for the advice, Ellie. I needed that."

Cami looked at the scoreboard. It read:

	R	H	E
Simms	3	5	0
Henderson	2	2	2

Pointing to the Blazers' line score, Cami said, "You're right, Ellie. Deuces are wild."

Because of rain, the title game was postponed for two days. That turned out to be a big break for Cami. Coach Thomas picked her over Kelly LeClerc to pitch for the championship against the Salem High Skyhawks.

"Cami, I want you to start on the mound today even though you've had only two days' rest," the coach said. "Give it everything you've got. I'll bring Kelly in the moment you get tired. I have a hunch you've got one more great pitching performance in you. Are you up to it?"

"I'm so up you'll need the space shuttle to bring me back down."

On the bus trip to the ballpark, Cami tried to mentally prepare for the biggest game of her life. She sat alone, gathering her thoughts. Above all, she wanted to settle her stomach, which was flip-flopping between anxiety and excitement. *This is it, my very last game as a high school player. I have a chance to make a mark for Simms and pitch for the state title. But Salem is a great team with lots of power hitters. What if I get shelled? Stop thinking like that.*

As the Eagles stepped off the bus, Cami sought out

Ellie's spirit. "Ellie, will you be with me? I really need you. You will be there, won't you?"

When they entered the locker room, Cami had her answer.

"Whew! What's that smell?" asked sophomore Georgette Bauer.

"It's patchouli oil!" shouted Cami, grinning broadly.

"There's only one girl on this team who ever wore that stuff," said Stacy.

Then, in unison, a half dozen girls shouted, "Ellie!"

"She's with us today, girls," declared Cami. "Can there be any doubt?"

From the moment Cami hurled her first pitch—after tugging at her unicorn earring for good luck—it was obvious she was on a mission. No batter could touch her blazing fastball. She dared the hitters to swing at it. Time and again, Stacy called for the change-up, but Cami shook her off, going with fastballs and drop balls instead. She retired the first eighteen batters in a row, ten of them by strikeout. Only one Skyhawk managed to hit the ball out of the infield, a lazy fly to right.

Meanwhile, the Eagles clung to a 2–0 lead on the strength of back-to-back doubles and a single in the fourth inning.

It's a superstition in baseball that if a pitcher is throwing a no-hitter, no one must ever mention it, because talking about the no-hitter will cause the pitcher to give up a hit. But as the end of the game neared, everyone—including Cami—knew she was fashioning not only a no-hitter but a perfect game. She needed three more outs to make high school history.

The fans were on their feet, cheering wildly as Cami walked to the mound. And then, a strange silence engulfed her. She stood motionless. Nothing could reach her ears—nothing but Ellie's wonderful voice inside Cami's head.

"The heck with superstition, Cami. You're throwing a no-no. Yeah, you're tired. But guess what? If you dig down deep enough, you'll find the extra strength to blow the ball past these bozos. When you need that one big payoff pitch, go with your change-up."

"But I gave up a homer on my change-up in the last game."

"Go with the change-up. I'll do what I can for you, because there's no way you can pull this off without help from your old batterymate. I want this championship just as much as you do. Maybe more. And I want the no-hitter too—even though it means giving up my patchouli oil. Remember the deal we made when we first met?"

Suddenly the cheers, shouts, claps, and whistles assaulted Cami's ears and jarred her back into the game. "Let's go, let's go." "Three up, three down!" "You can do it, Cami!"

On the first pitch, the leadoff batter, who was known for her power, laid down a perfect bunt between the pitcher's mound and third base. Caught by surprise, Cami broke late on the ball. But incredibly, the runner stumbled coming out of the batter's box. Third baseman Kathy Monroe charged in, picked up the ball barehanded, and pegged it to first on a bang-bang play. "Out!" yelled the umpire.

The next batter, Becky Langley, was Salem High's best hitter. On a 2–2 pitch, Becky caught hold of Cami's fastball and launched a towering drive down the left field line. The Simms fans groaned, knowing a home run would ruin the no-hitter and the shutout. But at the last moment, the ball curved foul by inches.

Cami blew a sigh of relief. On the next pitch, Becky sent a liner screaming back toward Cami's head. As Cami ducked, she blindly stuck out her glove and the ball slammed into the webbing for the second out. So much of the ball was showing that it looked like Cami was holding an ice cream cone.

The Eagles whooped for joy. Stacy called time and trotted to the mound along with the rest of the infielders.

"How did you ever catch that bullet?" asked Stacy.

"I don't know," Cami admitted. "It was like an invisible hand shoved my glove there before I had time to think about it." Pointing to the small patch bearing the number 2 on her sleeve, she added, "I think we know whose hand that was."

"One more!" declared Kelly. "That's all, Cami! One more and the title is ours!" The infielders patted Cami on the back, then went back to their positions.

The next batter worked the count to three balls and two strikes. A walk would spoil the perfect game and bring the potential tying run to the plate. Stacy called for a fastball. But Cami shook her off. The catcher signaled for a drop ball. But again, Cami nixed it. Stacy called time and ran back to the mound. "What's going on, Cami?"

"I'm going with the change-up," she whispered.

"But you haven't thrown one the whole game. Why now?"

"It's time. I know what I'm doing."

"Okay," said Stacy, as she trotted back behind the plate. Cami rubbed her unicorn earring. Then she wound up and let loose with her change-up. The batter, expecting a fastball, swung way too soon and whiffed at the pitch. The second the ball settled into Stacy's mitt, Cami leaped high in the air and gleefully screamed, "Yes! Yes! Yes!"

A perfect game and the state title!

The fans danced in the stands and shouted themselves hoarse as the Eagles piled on Cami, forming a wiggling heap of legs and arms on the pitching mound. When the pile finally unraveled, Cami punched her hands in the air. "Ellie, we won it! You and I and all our teammates. We're the state champions!"

An hour later the Eagles were still high from the happiness of victory. Showered and dressed, they were getting ready to leave when Stacy walked by Cami's locker.

"I sure do like your perfume, Cami. What's it called again?"

"Charlemagne. My aunt in France sends it to me every Christmas."

Only then did Cami realize that she hadn't put on any perfume yet. The bottle in her locker was still closed. She kissed her fingers and touched them to her unicorn earring. "Thanks for being there for me, Ellie. And thanks for sticking by our deal. I've always hated your patchouli oil."